Running Away to Home

Running Away to Home

You May Leave Home, but Home Never Leaves You

Ruby O'Gray

iUniverse

RUNNING AWAY TO HOME
YOU MAY LEAVE HOME, BUT HOME NEVER LEAVES YOU

iUniverse books may be ordered through booksellers or by contacting:

iUniverse
1663 Liberty Drive
Bloomington, IN 47403
www.iuniverse.com
1-800-Authors (1-800-288-4677)

ISBN: 978-1-4917-8600-0 (sc)
ISBN: 978-1-4917-8599-7 (e)

Library of Congress Control Number: 2016900433

Print information available on the last page.

iUniverse rev. date: 03/24/2016

I dedicate this book to my husband, Henry, for inspiration that he did not know he gave, and to my children: three daughters-Olivia, Samantha, Victoria, and my triplet sons, Gregory, Lewis and Edward, who taught me so much about the mentally challenged from their premature -asphyxiated births, and to my two granddaughters, Jasmine Simone and Amaia Renea, my siblings, Mattie, Christine, Edward, Paul and the late Anthony, Bill, and Grover, all of whom I love dearly. I also dedicate this book to the wonderful women I've known who no longer breathe life on this earth: My mother, Lucille, for her love and kindness, my Grandma Mattie Will Moore, for her love, the gift of humor, endurance, and imagination, my "gift" mother, Louise "V.V" Davis, who treated me just like her daughter-giving me love and encouragement.

CONTENTS

CHAPTER I

A Double

Kathleen's two older brothers, Brian and Derrick, were reluctant to let her play on their stickball team, but their best hitter, Charles, was under punishment for being *manish*: doing something a man might do, but little boys are only supposed to think about. Charles couldn't even sit on the porch and watch the game, let alone play, while the boys from the nearby Foote and Cleaborne Projects united with their Pontotoc Street boys to beat the tough Cynthia Street team. Charles was "the hope" of the Pontotoc Street kids. This particular summer, the teams were tied 3 games to 3, and this game would determine the winner of the neighborhoods. In desperation, the team's decision to use Kathleen in Charles' place was met with much opposition by all of the teams. It was unprecedented for a girl to do anything except watch, bring water, cheer, dust the bases, or hold the towels for the teams to wipe sweat or dirt from their faces. The guys had no choice but to use Kathleen. Though she was a good hitter and had very pretty girly legs to look at, they were much too short to compete for the fast paced run to the bases the Pontotoc team relied on Charles' to do. The team needed a home run, plain and simple.

Kathleen's two brothers had seen her put one over the fence many times when she was just playing for fun, and she was unaware that anyone was looking. Brian and Derrick wondered if Kathleen could do the same in a real game; with real pressure, so they convinced the rest of the team to let their sister play. Kathleen was nervous that she could not only be the first female to play and hit a homer for the team, but she might just be the last one to ever play ball with the Pontotoc Street Sluggers.

Later that night after the game, Kathleen curled up in her bed, pulled out the old ledger that her grandma's employer had thrown out, and began to write with her no. 2 pencil. A month ago when her grandma gave it to Kathleen she said, "Lawya," as she called him, "threw this out and I tore all ' his old work out of it so you can have clean pages to write on. 'Dis here book got a whole lot of long pages so you can write a lot." Kathleen was used to hand me downs and other used items from the people her grandma worked for. Kathleen wrote on the cover, My Dear Diary:

It is 11:14 at night, and this is1960, and I am almost 13 years old. My brothers Derrick and Brian and their friends asked me to play stickball. After begging them to let me do it, they said that they believed that I could hit far. For real the reason was that the best hitter, Charles Lincoln, was being punished for looking up a girl's dress at church with his nasty self. I almost hit him once for trying to put a mirror by my feet. I want the team to want me because I am a good hitter. They always say that my legs are too short to out run a bowlegged midget, but I can hit a ball as far as any boy!

Today I was supposed to prove to them what I could do, but today I cried. The first time I came up to bat, I was nervous and scared because the team was counting on me. I struck out. I could not believe it, but I did. That long armed Jabbo from Cynthia Street threw that ball too fast, and I swung and missed it twice before I tapped it and fouled. The other team laughed at me. Then the next time I came up to bat I missed the whole ball. I just wanted to run away from them all, but I couldn't. I had to stay. I got mad, and told myself that I could hit that ball. My last time up to bat I hit it! I hit that ball so hard, and everybody was cheering when it went over the fence. Suddenly, the ball splashed into a bucket where people behind our house lived. My Grandma said that they were drunks, and every Friday and Saturday they lit a big fire under a pot making that red stuff called *canned-heat. They were always loud and drinking and didn't have too much to do with anybody, but they liked all of my family, because my Mama gave the lady some clothes from Grandmama's white people. They don't cuss us out like they do everybody else on the street, because my Mama was real nice to them when the lady's husband second died. The next thing happened was that the ball boiled, and it turned into a rag! The lady took a colander and strained it from the pot, but that did not stop them from drinking that canned-heat! At least I hit a home run, but the team didn't care, because now they told me that I was off the team for losing the ball. I can hit hard, but one day when my legs grow long, I will outrun all of them, even all my brothers. If I could run fast, then I could get away with hitting my brothers and not get caught. But Mama ain't, I mean isn't (I don't have an eraser Dear Diary to take off the word ain't), but Mama will not let them hit me, anyway and

3

Grandmama will maul their heads if they do. I think that I just want to run sometimes even if I don't hit a home run. God did not give me long legs like my Mama. I don't want to play stickball ever again until I get older and grow long legs. By Kathleen-The End. P.S. If anybody reads this without my permission, they might go blind and never see for 40 days and 40 nights. (Maybe just 3 days and 3 nights) I am sorry, God, I did not mean that.

Kathleen reached 16 when her mother became gravely ill and she wrote about it in more old ledgers by the end of 1965. She wrote almost every day of that year until 1966 when as she boarded a Continental Trailways bus for the city so nice they named it twice. The bus was crowded, and the smell of some of the White passengers wet from the Virginia rain was all too familiar to Kathleen. She had spent many summers working with her grandmother in homes of southern white people, who, during the summer heat, hosed down their children who would then tread water throughout the house on the shiny hardwood floors that her grandmother had just waxed. Her grandmother whispered to the then 7 year old Kathleen, "Smell that? Most White folk smell like wet dogs when water hits 'em outside the tub; it's 'day hair.'" Her grandmother finished cleaning up everything in the house, spoke to the lady about how the children kept on messing up the floor and her having to keep on cleaning it. Perturbed, the white lady said something to her grandmother about Kathleen eating too much for lunch and bringing her grandchild to work every week. Kathleen's grandmother assured the lady that she would not be bringing Kathleen again, as she finished out the day. She left the house spotless, picked up her week's pay, walked out the door, and never came back. The ex-employer pleaded for weeks for Kathleen's grandmother to return; offering her more money, but she wouldn't budge. She said, "Because there is such a thang as respect, baby, and that's 'bout all I got, and they sho' nuff didn't act like they had none for me after all these years of scrubbing they dirty floors and funky ass draws. It's too many white folk want a house and kitchen magician like me. They know I'm honest, I'm clean, and I can cook good enough to make a pot sing. I know plenty; dey friends always asking me. Dey ' be glad for me to bring my grandbaby with me, and they ain't gon' pay no mind whatever one little ole colored girl eat, either. You got to show who you be, in this world, child; show who you be, or you n'er will git no respect."

The crowded bus triggered memories that Kathleen was leaving; escaping, in hopes of new and adventurous ones. Her hopes, for the most part, relied on unrealistic fantasies influenced by the television. The '40s movies, for example, like *On The Town* with Frank Sinatra, Gene Kelly, and an actor's name Kathleen could never remember, who played sailors on furlough in New York for 24 hours. They danced, sang, and found love all in one evening. Her experience would be similar, she thought, one that was magical and movie-like. Kathleen's thoughts about the North and South were like the Confederate and Union armies-very different. Aside from her Chicago-based great-uncles, Kathleen knew only Southerners. But she felt, with certainty, that northern whites would be sophisticated and not prejudiced. They would discover Kathleen's singing talent and help her gain fame and fortune. This bus ride brought Kathleen much needed distance from her home- the segregated, unsophisticated place where she was raised-Memphis, Tennessee, and from the memory of her mother's death, and anything else that made her unhappy. Feeling tired but relieved to be on the bus, she closed her eyes and tried to sleep, but visions of what prompted her to leave still cluttered her mind:

Seven months prior, Kathleen was walking aimlessly on the street very late at night near the hospital where her mother, Lucinda, had been admitted. The unsettling news prompted the late night walk. There was no phone in the house where her family lived, and the lady next door, Ms. Paine, came by to deliver the message from Aunt Mary that Lucinda had just passed. Kathleen immediately tore a piece of cardboard from a box and placed it in her shoes to cover the holes. She ran as fast as she could to the hospital that seemed miles away, to the screams of her family asking her to come back. The hospital was only about eight blocks from the dilapidated duplex where her family lived. Her stepfather, hearing the tragic news, had jumped up and down saying "Got damn, Got damn, Got damn"- careful not to use the Lord's name in vain, which her family was taught never to do. Kathleen ran so fast that she began to feel faint. Her short legs jumped over what seemed like endless puddles of water that formed from the trickling rain. The sooner she arrived at the hospital, Kathleen thought, there was some kind of mistake; of course her mother was alive. After all, Aunt Mary was always wrong about things or lying. Like the time that she insisted that a teenaged Kathleen had full breasts as a direct result of boys fondling them, or that men were not adjusting themselves, but pulled their pants in the middle to help their "thang" grow. Kathleen's brother, Brian, would joke that Aunt Mary was older than dirt, a liar, and always trying to act smarter than anybody in the family when she was really very stupid. Everyone in the family thought the same thing about her. Kathleen thought, "What did Aunt Mary really know about her mother, Lucinda? All she ever did was criticize her for having a house full of children. Kathleen wondered why Aunt Mary never offered to help them by driving them to the hospital or to help the family transport groceries when they shopped. After all, she was the only one in the family who always kept a car, and it would have helped Kathleen get back quickly to the house to tend to her little sisters and cook, then get back home quickly from the hospital when she visited her mother. Aunt Mary was just plain lowdown and mean, but her mother urged them to respect her and treat her well.

Kathleen suddenly stopped running and looked at her shoes. Her mother had told her before, "I don't want my pretty girl to come out here looking like this. You have to sit so no one knows that you have holes in your shoes. Keep your feet down flat on the floor," Lucinda demanded. Lucinda loved Kathleen so, and felt guilty that she could not provide for her. Kathleen had grown accustomed to blazers and skirts, clothes that fit well from the people her grandmother worked for, but Kathleen could not wear their oxford Catholic shoes, because her feet were bigger than theirs. Lucinda never wanted Kathleen to be embarrassed or to have the appearance of the poor little colored girl that she was. She knew that Kathleen's light complexion, big legs, and tiny waist were a magnet to the opposite sex. Before her mother became gravely ill, potential suitors discovered the secret to approaching Kathleen- it was her mother. When Lucinda would sit on the porch, guys would offer to buy her her favorite ice-cream, black walnut, or get her a

Double Cola, which helped them flatter the mother to keep company with her daughter. "That's really up to Katy, ya'll," she would say, "She is such a tomboy; I don't really know if she's interested." She was interested, but not as much as other girls her age. Kathleen was devoted to her mother, and whatever advice Lucinda gave her daughter, especially about men, was sacrosanct to Kathleen. Lucinda worried about her attracting the wrong kind of man, but the appearance of needing a man's help would mean trouble in the long run.

A sense of relief came over Kathleen as she thought about Aunt Mary, a mean "old fart" of a woman according to her stepfather's description. Her aunt seemed to delight in making others unhappy. Perhaps this was one of the worst lies she could have told- Lucinda dead?-Absurd, a word Kathleen loved to use from old movies that she watched. Unfortunately, the pondering about her mother ended when one of the night nurses came into view upon her arrival. She recognized Kathleen who emerged rain-drenched and breathless from the elevator of the William Bowld Hospital, and stood as if stuck to the floor for a moment before running toward her mother's room. The nurse had to physically restrain Kathleen from going in. Kathleen was inconsolable yelling repeatedly, "Is my Mama dead? The nurse was quiet. "Let me go! Let me go!" Kathleen cried. "I want to see my Mama; she told me to come back today; I want to see her now! Please! Please!" A lone male orderly held Kathleen as her legs buckled. He carried her into an empty waiting area and tried to console her. "Your mother slept away peacefully, Kathleen," the nurse said. "Now, you know Ms. Lucinda wouldn't want you to act this way, baby." They put a cold towel to her head and now tear-soaked red face, hoping Kathleen would calm down.

Her Aunt Mary was still there and offered to take her back home, but Kathleen refused. The nurse broke hospital policy, and allowed her relax until Kathleen left the hospital about half an hour later. She walked home slowly with steps that were reminiscent of a snail's crawl. By the time she reached home, the rain had stopped and suddenly, so did Kathleen. She looked up to the sky and made a vow to God that if cancer ever invaded her body she would fight it harder than her mother did. She would not let it kill her- SHE would live.

Reminiscing led to sleep for Kathleen, but she awakened when the bus came to an abrupt stop and someone yelled, "We're home." Kathleen didn't think the Greyhound would ever stop for a break. The restroom on the bus was just too nasty to use without alcohol to clean it; especially after an elderly lady kept announcing her bout with diarrhea while trotting up the isle. Sitting in the front seat of the bus next to her was Kathleen's friend, Dorothy, whose nickname was Shug, short for "Sugar." She had become Kathleen's best friend since her mother's death. Shug was a very heavy sleeper, so Kathleen had to shake her vigorously to wake her up. Each time Shug yawned, her tobacco chewing breath was in Kathleen's face. Kathleen wondered how or why in the world a 21 year-old woman could chew tobacco and like it. Although Shug never chewed it around the men she dated, she was not beyond doing so in public. Kathleen hoped that Dorothy would not embarrass her in front of the other passengers by biting into a plug and spitting the juice out of the window or in an old can, which she wash and carried everywhere.

With Dorothy's orchestration, they were on their way to New York, after having discussed a little matter of all

9

things "country" staying buried in the country-meaning left back in Memphis. Apparently, this did not apply to Dorothy's tobacco. Dorothy was originally from Greenwood, Mississippi, but moved to Memphis by the age of eight with her family of fourteen brothers and sisters. Like Kathleen, she never finished school, but not because she was parentless, but because she was known as fast and hardheaded. Books and school did not sit well with Dorothy, because she could read well, and she had sex on the brain. Despite these two facts, Dorothy was as kind as kind could be to anyone who was her friend, and a street-wise protector of Kathleen, who knew little about scams, traveling, or men. Dorothy was running away from Memphis just as Kathleen was. Only Dorothy was literally running away from painful memories- physical pain.

A few weeks before in Memphis, Dorothy had worked in the Harlem Restaurants as a short order cook, dishwasher, or whatever they needed. One evening, after her shift was over, she went outside and was kissing her man while he leaned against the side of his car. He was off work at 2 o'clock, and had come to take Dorothy home or somewhere. They were affectionately planning their next "date" when a city bus stopped near where they stood. A tall, vicious looking, coal-black skinned, heavy-set woman jumped off the bus and ran toward them. The woman had apparently announced her intentions while on the bus, because the driver di not drive immediately after the woman got off until a premeditated scenario was played out. Shug and the man were totally oblivious to what was about to happen.

Shortly afterwards, Kathleen received a call from the restaurant asking her to send a special cab to pick up Dorothy.

The cabbie was a man named Taylor, who drove for Little John Taxi and Dorothy told Kathleen that he was a family friend who would either charge her less fare or extend her credit on a ride. Kathleen called, left word with the dispatcher, and soon Taylor called back. He brought Dorothy to the rooming house that belonged to Kathleen's grandmother. She opened the door as Taylor held a scarred, teary-eyed Shug. Deep bloody fingernail scratches marked the side of her cheeks, arm, and neck, as she sobbed so pitifully. Although Dorothy was a woman with an enviable figure, she was not much to look at in the face. She had a protruding bottom lip, and her baby-like voice and slight lisp would become more obvious the more nervous Dorothy became. But men just really loved her. It was her "brick house" figure and that attention-getting high-pitched baby voice of hers that intrigued men most of the time. Old men were always asking if they could take care of her, while young ones sometimes enjoyed one night with Dorothy that led to their calling her back- usually to no avail. Dorothy appeared to not care if they came back or not, but was known to accept an invitation from what she called "pretty men" (high yellow). She knew that they weren't going to be serious relationships. Men also loved to dance with her, as she swayed sensuously on the dance floor, emphasizing her round, firm behind. Kathleen had heard a neighbor say, "You know what, men might put a sheet over Dorothy's head or turn out the lights not to look at her, but they sho'nuff talked about her bedroom capabilities." Kathleen thought about what her brother Derrick would have been called her- a "two-bagger," meaning that she was a woman that a man had to put two bags over her head to make love to her in case the first one came off. Shug also had a huge gap

11

between her pearly white teeth and a big flat-like nose, but her skin was enviably silky smooth, almost without blemish or scar. If there was anybody who didn't need a bruised face, it was Dorothy. Kathleen felt that Dorothy, in spite of her morals, did not deserve what happened to her in front of the restaurant. Dorothy really loved this bum of a guy, but they were an accident waiting to happen. By all accounts from their co-workers, it was the most one-sided fight that they had ever seen.

After the woman got off the bus, she approached Dorothy and the man she was with. The woman then took her big leather purse, and without warning, whacked her husband over the head with it. With every blow, she made noises like a wrestler in the ring. The big football player-looking garbage man moved quickly and got into the car leaving Dorothy without refuge. The woman snatched the human hair pinned down wig off Dorothy's head, pushed her against the car and proceeded to scratch her with her long well-manicured fingernails. Dorothy tried to defend herself, but could not see for the woman's fingers in her eyes. The woman then kicked her in the side and said, according to the waitresses in the restaurant, "I knew' I was gonna get a chance to beat your ass, you slimy ass bitch! Messing with my husband! You ain't gon' be fucking him or nobody else for a long time. 'What the hell' he see' in your ugly ass anyway?" While Dorothy was down, the enraged woman kicked her several times in and near her private. Fearing the death of his mistress, the boyfriend finally came to Dorothy's rescue. He grabbed his wife from behind and held her tightly yelling, "Come on baby, come on, please, that's enough now! Let's go!" With that, the woman yelled, "I'm gonna kill you and that bitch if I catch you with her again; you hear me?" The bus pulled off, and the man and woman got into the car, but not before the woman hocked and spat on poor Dorothy. She then threw Dorothy's wig on top of her while cursing her. The couple sped away as the woman threw a rock that she'd picked up at Dorothy as a last injury to insult. This was the man who Dorothy said made her stop messing around with anyone other men. This was the man who had her "nose open" so wide that a train could pass through it. That night Kathleen began nursing her friend's physical wounds. Three days later, the inside wounds left Dorothy with a decision- it was time to leave Memphis.

The bus was filled with some new faces as most of the old ones who sat in the back had gotten off at other stops. Kathleen was noticing how much better the bus smelled, when a pale freckled-faced white woman sat down on the isle seat across from her. The woman smiled at Kathleen and began eating a piece of chicken that she pulled from a greasy brown paper bag. The woman kicked off her shoes, humming while she ate. Dorothy had brushed her teeth and turned toward the window to look at the hills where little houses sat on top of green fields. Through the distance, Kathleen saw an almost identical view on the other side of the bus that continued for hours. To Kathleen, it was like traveling in a valley of fairy-tale like villages. Kathleen had never been past Arkansas, and this trip was beginning to frighten her more and more. They were rapidly approaching New York, and there was no turning back.

The red-headed woman had so many freckles on her face that they could have been mistaken for tattoos. She asked, "You girlth ' sthuth-sthers?' "No, ma'am, we're not sisters, we're uh, cousins," Dorothy replied. With a smile revealing several missing front teeth, the woman added, "Well, I'm going to visith my 'thithster in New York. Where are you going? "Ma'am we are not supposed to tell people anything. Our parents told us not to talk to strangers," Dorothy quickly injected. Kathleen was about to spill her guts. She never seemed to understand that unwritten rule her grandmother taught her about volunteering information to people and especially white folks. Her grandmother from time to time would say, "They always think that they are entitled to ask colored people our business, but you don't have to tell 'em, baby; slavery is over." The woman responded, "I wath juth trying to be friendly, girths, thath's all. Do you want thome of my 'thicken?" Simultaneously, the girls said "No, ma'am," as Kathleen added, "Thank you." The woman had the worst lisp Kathleen had ever heard; even Dorothy, who had a slight one herself, could hardly understand her. Maybe Kathleen forgot about telling her business, but she didn't forget about taking food from strangers. That was an absolute no, no. It was not that they did not like white people, but they both had been warned not to trust them, because they always betrayed colored people just when they began to trust them.

After stops in other towns and many runs to varied restrooms, the girls reached the sardine packed New York bus terminal. Kathleen was amazed how noisy, dirty and smoky everything seemed. They had been given papers with directions as to where the subway was and how to get to the agency that would help them find a job. This would be Dorothy's second time in New York, but Kathleen's first. Dorothy talked Kathleen into taking the trip when all means of salvaging their respective romances ended. It surprised

Kathleen how friendly New Yorkers seemed, as a man grabbed her bag right out of her hand and asked her where she was going. "To the subway and then right here," showing him her instructions on the paper she held. The short stubby man smiled and said, "I'll help you find it, little lady; youse girls got to be careful in the Naked City." "We know where it is, thank you," Dorothy said, and quickly snatched the suitcase away from him. "Girl, you can't talk to everybody in New York; I done told you," Dorothy whispered. Kathleen replied, "Shug, he seemed nice and wanted to help." "Yeah, and so did Jack the Ripper just before he cut some woman's guts out. I've been here before-you ain't."

Getting a token and waiting for the subway was a complete culture shock for Kathleen. Passing wooden telephone booths that she had never seen at home, Kathleen opened one, only to find a very dirty man reeking of urine, who immediately yelled, "Close the damn door!" Kathleen began to wonder why she was in this town with awful nasty people like that, but Dorothy's announcement of the subway's arrival interrupted that train of thought. Jumping on and finding a seat together, the girls looked at the instructions they had in their purses that would lead them to Manhattan. The lady at the agency in Memphis had been very thorough with them, but did not seem to be concerned as much with their ages as Shug had suggested they would. The subway tunneled rapidly as Kathleen watched the odd-looking people occupying the car. She was afraid, but determined not to show it to Dorothy. She wanted to cry, for the lie that brought her to this place seemed awfully insignificant now. The pangs of hunger to see her grandmother and other family members were increasing. She wondered if she'd ever go back home, or if she'd find her place in life right there in New York City. Kathleen began to talk herself into reasons why the move was right. After all, why shouldn't she go? Her mother was dead, and the only people left who cared about her were her brothers and sisters and of course, Dorothy, her silly, man-crazy, but streetwise and loyal friend. Besides, it was as if her life had become like a baseball game; striking out three times in Memphis. Kathleen needed to make a move, a geographical change, and a healing of her heart. At the same time, Kathleen thought that while she had been "down" in the south, she had nowhere to go but "up" in the north; in New York. Still the recurring visions of home always seemed to come when Kathleen closed her eyes to sleep, always centered around the greatest loss of her life-her mother.

"That sure was a nice funeral," Aunt Mary declared, bringing unpleasant looks from other family members as she entered her sister's house. Kathleen's brother, who made light of every word Aunt Mary uttered, whispered to Kathleen, "That old woman would go to funerals everyday just to smile at dead people and pretend to get happy and shout. Too bad she doesn't know that she, herself, is dead and came back to haunt all of us." Kathleen grabbed her brother and went to the other side of the room so no one would see them laugh to the point of Kathleen shaking. Aunt Mary reacted, "Those poor little children; look at them shaking and grieving for their mother." Kathleen's two older brothers were in the military- the Navy and the Army. They wanted to help their sister, but they had just finished boot camp and could barely help themselves. Aunt Mary again volunteered information at a time when people, other than family, were present. "I was glad I had a thousand dollars saved to help with the funeral, but somebody ought to have had some insurance on Lucinda from the get go. That's why I won't marry nobody; these country ass men don't understand nothing about how to take care of family." Kathleen thought, "Why couldn't it have been Aunt Mary instead of my mother? Her heart is as black as the dress she's wearing, and she is not a good person." Kathleen quickly asked God to forgive her for the thought and held on to her brother, Brian.

Lucinda's mother was Aunt Mary's sister-Kathleen's grandmother. After the funeral, all of the family ate at the rooming house her grandmother owned. Aunt Coreen was Lucinda's aunt too, by marriage to her Uncle Alfred- who they all knew as classy, but a drunk nevertheless. Coreen walked over to comfort Lucinda's husband and said loudly, "I was only too glad to give her that grave, Rufus. I loved that child. She certainly was put away nicely. I know how hard it's been on ya'll financially." Then she began to cry as she said, "Lucinda was really a good woman." Kathleen sat looking at all the hugging and concern each member seemed to have for her mother. In the corner near the gas heater was a large decorated box with a big bright red ribbon wrapped around it. Kathleen walked over, read the card and smiled, as it had her classmates and ex homeroom teacher's name on it. It was filled with can goods and an envelope with twenty-six dollars in it. She took it and gave it to her grandmother, who then gave it back to her and whispered, "Keep it, baby." There was a note attached telling Kathleen how much they missed her and wanted her back in school. She had quit the eleventh grade to take care of her ailing mother and planned to return at her mother's insistence.

Whenever her classmates would see her they would put on a smile to bolster her feelings, but behind her back, they pitied her, because Kathleen was missing out on all the fun that they were having at school. This would confirm how poor Kathleen really was, since it was always the neediest family that got baskets and donations from the school. The poorest families were always pitied in school, but not ridiculed. It was not that the other kids were wealthy- most families that lived near Booker T. Washington High School stayed in the projects. Then, in the 60s, the projects were considered one of the cleanest, safest, and more popular housing for black people; it was a place that Kathleen and her family lived near, but not in, excluding them from being what was known as the "project elite."

The burning question that no one raised was resting on Kathleen's mind, and about to burst from her mouth. What was gonna happen to her? Kathleen was a teenager who Cousin Fannie had always loved. She spent the night at her home from time to time, and Fannie was always so nice to her, but the last time she spend the night at cousin Fannie's, her young hairdresser boyfriend stayed over and sat up until after one in the morning talking to her and styling Kathleen's long hair. He was about thirty and Fannie was at least ten or fifteen years older than he was. She told Kathleen that he was just a friend who just happened to sleep in Cousin Fannie's room. She never had Kathleen over again; it seemed sudden, but Cousin Fannie just didn't want Kathleen around anymore. This was strike one, Kathleen thought, for places to live and return to school.

Kathleen was determined not to be left with her stepfather, because she remembered how he had lied to her mother about Earl, her brother's friend and classmate, who had a crush on her. He said that Earl was "feeling all over her" when he walked in the kitchen while Kathleen as doing her homework. He did not want him or any boy coming to the house. This was a difficult option, because Kathleen was torn between staying with her younger brothers and sisters and asking another relative if she could stay with them. Imagining her mother's voice, Kathleen thought about what she always said, "If something happens to me, don't you worry about your sisters and brothers; they will be alright. You go and live with your Grandmama, you hear? Your stepfather is a man, just like anybody else- and he really ain't your blood." This became apparent ever since Kathleen developed into an attractive young woman. Since Lucinda's illness, he also did not care whether Kathleen went to school or not, just as long as there was dinner on the table when he got home from work and the other children taken care of- his children, his blood. When angry or trying to make a point, her stepfather would mention that three of her Mama's children were not his. As the three were growing up, he had been like a daddy to all of them, but this gradually changed with the boys becoming young men, and Kathleen was becoming a young lady. Kathleen thought that she would end up at her grandmother's house, even though her mother's brother, who lived there, was notorious for bringing home young women for sex; women close to Kathleen's age.

When the family gathered to plan Lucinda's funeral, no one mentioned what was going to happen to the children, so Kathleen just blurted out a question for a quick answer. "Do I go home with you tonight, Aunt Coreen, or do I stay at Grandmama's?" All who were in the room looked around at each other, but no one answered. Suddenly Kathleen's stepfather spoke very firmly, "I'm gonna need somebody to stay with these children so I can go to work. You got to be here, girl! We got to pack up to move next week 'cause we just got the letter to move into the Fowler Homes." The Fowler Homes were some of the best looking projects in Memphis, and Kathleen had filled out an application at her mother's request a year before her death. Lucinda's wish was to live in the projects for better economic conditions for her daughter; for her whole family. She could then afford to buy Kathleen some new clothes, and she wouldn't have to wear hand-me-downs.

Jimmy Lee attended Kathleen's mother's funeral. He loved Kathleen, and said it all time in a tone that Kathleen hated- like an old slave-like voice. Jimmy was a big old black as night strapping country boy who knew how to drive a truck, but could hardly write his name. Actually, most girls described Jimmy Lee as tall, dark, and handsome, and while he was that, Kathleen only spent time with him because she was lonely and for Lucinda's sake. Jimmy didn't talk about anything except the country or work; just as ther stepfather always did, being raised on an Arkansas farm. While he greatly admired Negroes with an education and those who played sports, especially baseball, her stepfather didn't think either would help women. He believed their place was cooking, cleaning, and having babies. Kathleen wondered why her mother seemed bent on a mission to find her a proper young man. When Jimmy Lee asked Kathleen to marry him within days after her mother's death, he whispered to her at the Wake, "Ms. Lucinda told me to ask you if something happened to her." Jimmy got down on both knees and said, "Yo' know I love ya', Kath-a-leen, and I will work hard and take good car' o' you. I loved Ms. Lucinda like a mother, and I think she loved me like a son. I promised her that I would take care of you; so what you gon' say?" Kathleen was not even tempted, since the thought of having more than a kiss with Jimmy was uninviting. Kathleen liked kissing Jimmy, something he seemed good at, but she knew that there was more that he wanted from her, and he wasn't gonna get it. She wanted more from life than Jimmy could ever offer. Shortly before her mother died, Jimmy told Kathleen that he used to always go home aching after seeing her. He would say, "I can't stand kissing ya too much, Kat-a- leen; I like it, but it really ain't he'ping my manly hood none." Kathleen worked up enough nerve to tell her mother what Jimmy said, and she wondered why he was always in pain and looking swollen as big as a cantaloupe in his pants as he walked hom. Her mother replied, "Just don't kiss that boy so much, Kathleen; men, well, men can't hardly help what they do sometimes when they get like that. You don't want him to think that you are teasing him, do you?" Kathleen understood, took her mother's advice and pecked Jimmy Lee on the cheek or hugged him from then on.

Despite the "no" on the marriage proposal, Jimmy still hung around, and helped her family move into the Projects, but a whole month had gone by, and Kathleen's stepfather did not want to talk about her going back to school in the Fall. He only talked about what the other children needed, and what she had to do for them. Jimmy Lee soon completely stopped coming around. Kathleen found out later on that it was at her stepfather's insistence that he did so that

Kathleen could get back to her books and school. Kathleen realized that Daddy Rufus was never going to consider her as anything but a nursemaid for the family. He would then block any man who would come after her. Kathleen longed to do some of the normal fun things any seventeen-year old would want- to dance, see her old school mates, or sing; things she had not done for a long time. Jimmy could not dance, and probably never would. She gathered that from the times she and Jimmy had spent together, which consisted of just watching television, listening to the radio, or talking about the country while holding her hand. Kathleen spent the rest of the time trying to stop Jimmy Lee from lifting her straight up in the air; she thought it was some kind of common country practice, because his whole family did the same thing, too. Jimmy treated her like a doll or some kind of toy. Kathleen knew that she had to make a change and it had to happen soon.

It was not a difficult decision for Kathleen to agree to go out on a double date with Cherita, a half black- half Mexican girl who she grew up with, but she was street-wise and had a wild streak that could not be tamed. She was a year younger than Kathleen, and had long since given up virginhood. Her grandmother raised her and ran a well-known gambling and transom house that probably contributed to Cherita's misguided wisdom of life. Kathleen was soon to be 18, and the desire to escape from the duties of housekeeping and mothering were strong. Cherita lied, and told Mr. Rufus that she and Kathleen were going to the movies with her cousins, and that she would have her back before midnight. It was a Friday night, and her stepfather reluctantly agreed. Kathleen put on the figure-hugging black dress that she had borrowed from Cherita to wear to her mother's funeral. While looking in the mirror, Cherita commented on Kathleen's enviable figure and flat tummy. Cherita had skinny, hairy legs, and large breasts, but no girl could compete with her strikingly beautiful half-Mexican slightly freckled face. Kathleen buckled a wide patent leather belt to accent her small waist, hooked the stockings to her garter belt, and put on the black patent leather spiked high heels that her grandmother had brought home from her "white people." Kathleen was like her mother was as a young woman-stacked like a finely built statue, only Kathleen was oblivious to the real problems that came with looking like that.

The cousins, who Cherita spoke of turned out to be two older guys of about thirty, who took them to a movie and dancing at a friend's house party where they played cards. Later on, the men left Kathleen and Cherita in the car while they walked into the seedy looking building called the Eureka Motel- a place that looked almost like the rooming house her grandmother owned. After entering, the ladies sat and had sodas, while the men had beers. Soon, they were led to their respective rooms by an attendant. Not aware of the exact reason why she was there or what part of town she was in, Kathleen quickly found out the real purpose for the room. She politely sat in a chair all night and fought Larry's advances. To his disappointment, no amount of persuasion could get her to take off her clothes. She told him that she would beat his brains out with her shoe if he came near her, and she was not playing either. Just before dawn, the men met in the hall, and Kathleen heard them deciding that this was a lost cause, and took the girls back to Cherita's house. Kathleen finally slept when she got there and returned home around 10am in a cab driven by Cherita's real life cousin. As soon as she entered the house, Kathleen was met with the hand of her stepfather across her face and a loud, "You 'ho'! Your Mama ain't cold in the grave and you fucking around already!" Kathleen tried to explain what happened, but he would not listen. He yelled, "Shut the hell up and get the fuck outta here!" Cherita had ridden back with her, and they both ran upstairs and packed Kathleen's clothes into an old suitcase and a brown Easy Way Food Store bag with double handles. Her stepfather came upstairs and told her if she could not do what he said she had to get her ass out of his house. Overlooking the tears and pleas from her little sisters and brothers, she finished packing. On the way down the stairs, her stepfather grabbed her arm, causing Cherita to react harshly with, "Take your fucking hands off her! If you hit her again, Mr. Rufus, I'll call the po-lice, 'cause you gon' have to hit me, too! Kathleen snatched her arm away, as he kept shouting and cussing at her, calling her names. Kathleen looked back at her sisters crying and left for Cherita's house. She went next door and called her Grandmother, who was at work, but told Kathleen where the key was. Fortunately, she lived within 30 minutes walking distance from Cherita. Kathleen knew that she would never return to the Fowler Homes; to her brothers and sisters. As time passed that day, Kathleen found herself becoming increasingly angry with her mother for leaving her alone; leaving her in this predicament.

Kathleen's grandmother was all too glad to have her come and live in her rooming house to keep it tidy and report on the tenants, who were all men; out of town construction workers or sometimes traveling musicians. Occasionally, when her Grandmother knew that the tenants' paydays might bring women in her house, she would suggest that Kathleen spend the night at Cherita's house. Kathleen was soon introduced to Cherita's friend, Dorothy. Cherita had met her at a dance the year before, and Dorothy and she would spend lots of time together. On alternate weekends, the girls would meet at Cherita's and alternate spending the night between Cherita's and Kathleen's place; usually when Kathleen's grandmother would have to stay on at one of her ill "white lady's" houses to make extra money. Kathleen liked this arrangement since she'd be with friends, and her grandmother would always give her money for keeping the house clean. Kathleen had plans of going to night school or getting a GED, and the money would help. Kathleen also agreed to work at the chain of Harlem House Restaurants as a dishwasher and swing shift girl at night, not to have her grandmother spend all of her money on her needs. If there was nothing else that she could do, Kathleen could cook and clean. But she still longed to meet young men and spend time with a boyfriend like other girls. Kathleen and Dorothy, being a little older than Cherita, became close friends, and Kathleen shared her wish to meet a young man. Little did she know that her wish was about to come true.

Dorothy got hired at a popular place where carhops worked, and after a couple of weeks, she took Kathleen with her to work to meet the boss, hoping she would get hired too. "There are some real cute guys that come here, and all you got to do is wear a little more make-up and your clothes a little tighter, and you will get hired. Girl, with your bright skin, you will have tips coming out 'your ears," Dorothy advised. The next night, Kathleen used her Grandmother's sewing machine, took up a pair of her pants so they'd fit a little tighter, and told her uncle that she was going to stay at Dorothy's. She knew that this would give him an opportunity to have one of his sex girls over while she was away, so he handed her five dollars when Kathleen told him that she'd be staying at Dorothy's that night. That was the night Kathleen met him-Ernest. She noticed him peripherally, as he was sitting in his car watching her walk across the lot with Dorothy. She was trying to teach Kathleen the art of getting tips, when he yelled for her to come to his car. He smiled and asked if she worked there, and she replied "No, not yet." She went inside the building; he soon followed her and sat down at a table. He stared at her until she became embarrassed. He soon went over to the table where she was and asked if he could sit down. He had a glass in one hand and a bottle of beer in the other. Kathleen was drinking a cherry-coke, and shaking from the presence of this tall, slim, not necessarily handsome, but magnetic man. He was almost as black as a lump of coal man, and he stared at Kathleen until she missed her mouth when trying to sip from a straw. They began to talk, and Kathleen became more comfortable as time went on. Her lesson with Dorothy as a potential car hop just ceased. The drive-in restaurant was about to close when he asked if he could drive Kathleen and Dorothy home. Dorothy quickly said yes, as she could not get in touch with Taylor, the cab driver, to take them home. After Dorothy thanked him, she excused herself and went into the house, leaving the two of them alone. They sat in the driveway on Greenwood Street reminiscing about both of their mothers passing on, music, sports and books. Kathleen's mother always encouraged her to read anything about everything, which included the Book of Knowledge, the Encyclopedia, Reader's Digest, National

Geographic, Playboy, the Bible, and any other book that her grandmother could bring home from the people she worked for. Kathleen used to get books from the neighborhood Library to read and become more informed. She even looked at the Playboy books and admired the beautiful nude women, hoping that she could look like them- flawless and pretty- and still be a "good girl."

Ernest looked at his watch and noticed that they had talked nearly fours. He said that he had to be at work by eight and needed to leave, then he kissed her ever so gently. That kiss turned into many more until the morning rays from the sun beamed on the windshield and ultimately on their faces. It was almost five o'clock, and they could barely separate themselves. The way Ernest's long and muscular arms seemed to wrap around and comfort her made Kathleen feel safer than she ever had since before the death of her mother. Kathleen gave Ernest Dorothy's telephone number before she went inside the house. Wide-eyed now, she was unable to sleep for hours. The Harlem Restaurant had called for her to work the swing shift that morning, but she couldn't- she had missed the call while outside and would have to have arrived at seven to work. Kathleen could not stop smiling as she sat down in the living room; she absolutely could not get Ernest out of her mind. He was definitely impressively sexy the way his deep voice seemed to roll off compliments. Kathleen thought about how this man had stirred up things inside her head; inside her body that she had never felt. She thought that if Ernest were a dance, his body was certainly doing a tango with her mind. Kathleen had kissed only four guys by the time she was seventeen, and that was as far as things went. For the most part, it was out of curiosity or

27

mimicking the kisses she had seen in old Clark Gable, Joan Crawford movies. No one had ever blown in her ear, bit her ear lobe, kissed her with such tenderness, while rubbing the small of her back consistently. She finally got in bed, closed her eyes and thought about how much they had in common. They both had lost their mothers, they both had step-parents in their lives that they didn't particularly like, and they both seemed lonely. Here was a young man alone at a drive-in restaurant, with no woman in his nice white Impala. Kathleen pulled out the long old ledger and wrote, "if this were a baseball game right now, I would call it the Ernest Inning, and I had just tasted the sweetness of a high pop fly that sent me running in a direction I had never gone before-a direction that I wanted to hit again."

The subway seemed to convert to what looked like a train as Kathleen and Dorothy actually got off on the top of a building. Following the directions on the paper, they walked to the four-story office building, and were met upstairs by a small Italian woman who sounded like the people Kathleen had seen on TV in *The Honeymooners* with Jackie Gleason. The woman was pleasant and smiled as she asked, "Now which one of you is Minnie and which is Dorothy?" Dorothy took charge-answering immediately- "I'm Dorothy and this is Minnie. Could we have a drink of water please, we have been riding for a long time?" "Certainly," she replied. "There's water over there in the cooler. I have some papers for you to sign as a formality and a few more things to do, and I'll be with you in a minute. Oh, please sign here that you arrived safely? It's just a formality. There were several clauses to each contract, so just give me a moment. Make yourselves comfortable." As soon as the woman left, Dorothy asked, "You didn't lose the social security card, did you?" "No, I didn't," Kathleen answered nervously. "I hope she doesn't find out. I just know something is going to go wrong."

Before they left, the girls were told at the Memphis agency that they needed to be at least eighteen to get the job. Dorothy was old enough, and luckily Kathleen's birthday was coming up in less than a week and a half. In order for Kathleen to go, she had to have identification on her age, so Dorothy devised a plan to get her some credentials. Days before they left, they went to a friend's house named Minnie, who lived on Olive Street with her sister and brother in-law. This was important to Dorothy's scheme as she was always trying to help Minnie find a job. Minnie hated living with her relatives and needed a job to move out- but more importantly, Minnie was twenty one. Country Minnie, as Dorothy described her, willingly handed her social security card after hearing Dorothy's promise to get her a job with a new factory business that was coming to town. Dorothy convinced Minnie that the employers had to have an identification of some sort to process people for the job. Since this was a way to ensure a job before the general public knew about it, Minnie would be guaranteed to have one. Dorothy could always be resourceful, if given the time to think things out. The naïve Minnie believed Dorothy; giving Kathleen a social security card. "I'm going to hell," Kathleen said, "I just know I'm going to hell. A lie will travel all around the world, while the truth is just getting its boots on." Dorothy looked at Kathleen and asked, "What the hell has that got to do with using that social security card? "That means if you tell a lie on someone, it will travel quicker than the truth?" "Then its traveling time, cause we got to lie," a nervous Kathleen replied, then pleadingly added, "They are going to put me in jail as soon as they find out I am not Minnie." Dorothy declared right then and there to call Kathleen Minnie as much and as soon as they left the real Minnie's house.

While sitting in the office and waiting, Kathleen thought about how she got to the agency. If it had not been for Dorothy, she would never have seen the section in the paper and gone to the ABC Maids office on Second Street in Memphis: "You girls have I. D.? We don't take clients with criminal records." The woman at the agency was very business-like. "We can't send you there without I. D. and we won't send you with a rap sheet," she said. "No, Ma'am, we have never been in jail," Dorothy quickly responded. "Here's our identification- give her yours Kat-Minnie. We always call my cousin Minnie Kat – it's a nickname." The wise woman said, "Yeah, well don't slip up and make that mistake up there, Dorothy. People might think that you are lying about who you are, you understand? I see that you are 21 and Minnie Kat is twenty one. You look older than your cousin, uh… Minnie is it? Kathleen answered, timidly "Yes, Ma'am." Then suddenly, as if a bomb had fallen in the room, the lady asked. "When were you born, Minnie?" The girls looked at each other and just as Dorothy was about to say something, Kathleen blurted out- "February 18, 1945, Ma'am. I was told that it was a night birth by my family back in back in Mississippi." Dorothy was astonished and added, "That's exactly what I was told. Where do we sign, ma'am, we want to go to New York as soon as possible." Kathleen had used a country girl type of voice and was ever so convincing

30

in her manner. The girls were told to come back and pick up their tickets, $16.50 each for food, and the directions to the agency in the city. Kathleen thought, they'd be gone in two days, they had two days to change their minds, work things out and stay with the men they loved, or two days to never come back again.

Kathleen had a habit of comparing her life to her favorite sport- baseball. Sitting in this New York agency, Kathleen thought about what happened while in the agency back home. She had sat filling out papers thinking about the 3 strikes that led her to start running from home, the south, to parts unknown, the north, New York, in hope of scoring a homerun. The woman soon returned with two envelopes informing them that their first potential clients were on their way. The girls were about to be separated, but she told them that she would try and keep the girls in contact, but it would be difficult. Kathleen was quite upset with this information and told the lady that if she did not hear from her cousin Dorothy within a week, she would definitely be going back home. There was a 30-day trial period for both employer and employee- something they had not been told by the agency in Memphis. Money could be lost by both agencies if the girls left before the trial period was up. Kathleen was very uneasy about not being able to contact Dorothy, and threatened to go back home. The woman agreed to tell them within the week, but Dorothy had other ideas while waiting to meet potential employers.

It was a beautiful day in the city, Kathleen thought, as she looked outside the office window at the shiny black new Continental being parked. A short, very well dressed woman

31

got out and entered the building; soon there was a knock on the front office's door. About ten minutes later, the woman entered where Kathleen and Dorothy sat. The lady was very cordial during the introduction- "Hello, I'm Mrs. Fasse, Betty Fasse;" extending her hand. The girls reciprocated, exchanged a few pleasantries; then the woman proceeded to choose one of them for hire. Kathleen picked up her bag and said goodbye as she hugged Dorothy, who whispered in her ear, "Find out where I am." As they took the elevator down to the car, a sense of awkwardness came over Kathleen, for this was a white woman who liked to touch, was less than five feet tall, and about forty- five or fifty years old. She talked nonstop and with great emphasis on every verb: "I hope that you'll like us. You certainly are a pretty girl. I don't know if the agency told you about us, but there are three in my family-my husband Aaron, my son, little Teddy and me. I have a daughter too, Trish, but she doesn't live with us anymore- she's married almost a year now, and expecting, God bless. Oh, she was married before though, I mean not married to someone else, I mean married before she got pregnant. You don't have any children do you?" "NO!" Kathleen answered quickly, startled by the question; "No-ooo Ma'am, I'm not married." Mrs. Fasse laughed and said, "I was just asking, you know. My friend's housekeeper left her children in Alabama, I think, to come to help her family, you know, send money home, and she had two children, I think. I am so glad that you don't have any, but that doesn't mean that you won't find a husband while you're here and leave us. Oh, but a lovely girl like you has lots of time for those things, right?" Kathleen almost answered, but Mrs. Fasse did not give her a chance to open her mouth before she was rattling off again. Kathleen put her bag in the trunk of the Continental and stood near the back door for Ms. Fasse to unlock it so that she could get in. Mrs. Fasse asked, "Why are you standing there? The front door is open; Minnie; get in." Seeing how puzzled Kathleen looked, Mrs. Fasse added, "Oh, we don't hold to those old ways you're used to down south, Minnie. You can sit in the front seat like anyone else." Mrs. Fasse continued to talk without interruption for over ten minutes when suddenly she said something right out of left field, "Bet you couldn't guess who my favorite singer was? Kathleen answered, "No Ma'am, I...I can't." Ms. Fasse continued, "The one, the only, silky voiced, Nat King Cole!" Kathleen laughed, as this was the first confirmation that she was really in the north. Imagine, she thought, white folks down home seeing her ride in the front seat, laughing, and white folk telling more of their business than asking a lot about hers. Times were changing, Kathleen thought, and so would she. But, she was now Minnie, riding in the front of a big old long car with a white woman driving and about to make $60 a week! A smile came over Kathleen's face that slowly changed to trembling lips and water-filled eyes. Mrs. Fasse looked at Kathleen, reached inside her patent leather purse for a tissue, and asked, "Homesick?" Kathleen nodded her head, and the floodgates opened. Mrs. Fasse hugged Kathleen and assured her that she would get the information about her cousin Dorothy's placement within the week. Mrs. Fasse sensed Minnie's pain and relief in her tears, and told her, "It's going to be all right, Minnie, it really is." Kathleen thanked her. As they started back up the highway, Kathleen knew what made her cry-the loss of her mother, the loss of love, the hurt and wrong impression from her grandmother, and what she hoped would not be another loss, her friend

Dorothy. With all the losses also came tears of relief that she was finally away from all the unhappiness back home and on her way to a place dominated by new kind of white people- Jews on Long Island. Kathleen's mind began to wander during the long ride- wander about home, Ernest, and why she had to leave her grandmother's house.

Months before New York, and several weeks after the passing of her mother, Kathleen and Ernest saw each other every other night of the week and weekends. One weekend, Ernest left with some friends and traveled to St. Louis, Missouri to see a game of his favorite sport- baseball. He promised Kathleen that he would be back the next day, so he urged her to have very little fun without him. Little did Kathleen know that a vicious lie was about to be told that would cause her great pain, and the loss of her respect from someone she loved very much.

Kathleen had lived at her Grandmother's rooming house filled with male tenants. Women were frequent visitors on the weekends; especially when the men got paid. Almost all of the men came from the East Tennessee area, and at least once a month they traveled home to be with their families. They lived near each other, leaving the house devoid of tenants. One weekend, all of the tenants left leaving Kathleen and her Uncle Walter. With Ernest gone, Kathleen's invited her friend Dorothy to spend the night. Walter was stinky drunk and made several passes at Dorothy, which led Kathleen to ask him to leave and walk it off or she'd call her Grandmother. Upset, her uncle left. Dorothy, could have handled him, but Kathleen knew that even though he was almost 40 years old, he still feared his mother.

The girls planned a night of conversation, manicures, petti-cures, watching TV, and doing their hair. An hour and a half or so passed when the conversation arose about Kathleen's C cup breast over Dorothy's A cup. The girls walked into the bedroom, looked in the mirror, and Kathleen showed Dorothy how to add tissue under her breast to make them look larger. This led to Dorothy giggling uncontrollable, who was very ticklish. Soon the girls were tickling each other and laughing all over the bed, with Dorothy topless and wearing panties, and Kathleen in her bra and pajama bottoms. Just then the door opened with Uncle Walter and a young woman who had gone to school with Kathleen. The girls rushed into the bed to cover themselves with the bedspread. There were two full sized beds in the room. Strict orders were given that absolutely no one should sleep in her Grandmother's bed or sit on it. Her uncle said nothing to them, but early the next morning, Kathleen's grandmother surprised everyone by showing up before seven in the morning demanding that Kathleen follow her to the back of the house. She very directly pointed her finger in Kathleen's face and said, "If you'a bulldagger, you gon' have to get the hell outta my house! I have always loved you, but I ain't putting up with no shit like this! Don't nobody in our family go that way! You running around with that gal, Dorothy, and I heard that she'll go with anything, anybody- man or woman. You wa'n't raised like that! Now you- (pointing at Dorothy) gon' have to leave, 'cause my son say you been after him everytime you come here. And I ain't gonna be running back and forth to see what you doing. Your mother would rise up from her grave and die again if she knew you done turned that way, Kathleen!" No wonder you been lying on Jr. 'bout women- he caught you dead to right."

Kathleen was so hurt, because her grandmother had never spoken to her that way, and she had hardly ever lied to her family; especially her Grandma. Kathleen suddenly became sick to the stomach and ran to the bathroom to throw up. Ever since she was a little child she had a temper, and whenever she tried to contain it she would get physically ill. Kathleen went marching into her uncle's room, where a woman was still in his bed, and asked him why he lied on her. Kathleen hadn't done anything that she was being accused of, but she could not understand how her Uncle Walter could lie like that, or how her grandmother could believe him. He arose from the bed; his burly body exposing his scaly feet and rusty legs. He coughed that early morning cough of heavy drinkers and smokers and answered, "You need to quit lying, I saw ya'll. I know a guy who knows a cab driver that told him and he told me. Everybody knows that girl is funny, and she dragging you down her funny ass life with her. She' trying to turn you out!' Feeling all over your titties, sleeping in the same bed! Why yawl got to sleep together, when Mama's big old empty bed 'right next to you? Kathleen defended Dorothy which made matters worse- "Naw, she didn't! I don't know nothing about no cab driver, but don't you think that she would have said something to me if she had been like that? And you know that Grandmama don't like nobody in her bed." Her Grandmother quickly added, "Yeah, but you know that I ain't never cared about you using nothing I had, Kathleen. Now I felt sorry when this here girl got beat up, but she' got to go. You can stay, but you got to repent of your sins. You got to go to church with me, get some holy water, blessed oil or something; get the devil rebuked from your body, and let the Bishop lay hands on you. Your soul ain't saved if you doing that kind of shit- it's a…a…uh-bomunation (abomination)." Kathleen countered, "And what about your soul and Uncle Jr's? He's a liar and you ain't no more than what Cherita's grandmother is. You let everybody come in here with these men and do what they want as long as they pay you, and you let him bring any stinky, nasty, slutty woman in here that he wants, and I'm the one getting put out for nothing? If you think that I'm like that, Grandmama, then I don't want to be around you; you ain't got to put me out-I'm going!" Kathleen began pulling clothes from the drawer and the shift-a-robe yelling, "Dorothy, call Taylor; and I ain't never coming back here as long as I live! And you, you make me sick, Uncle Walter! Ever since Dorothy turned you down, you' been out to get her and me. Grandmama, I never would have thought that you would do this to me. Never! I ain't never coming here, and I ain't calling you, either!"

The woman who was in the bed with her uncle had put on her clothes by now. Kathleen's grandmother lit into the woman, giving her a good tongue lashing about sleeping in her house. She held onto the woman's dress as she was trying to sneak out the door. Her grandmother turned, changing her voice to an almost tender level, and told Kathleen that she had too smart of a mouth, and she wasn't gonna have her talking to her like that. Her grandmother, feeling the impact of what Kathleen said, gave her and ultimatum. "You come back whenever you' ready if you repent and let Bishop lay hands on you." Then her grandmother turned around and cursed her son, and threw the girl out of the door. Deep down, she knew that her Grandmother was reacting to her son's bringing a woman in her house, but Kathleen was hurt and wanted nothing to do with her grandma right then. This was strike two to Kathleen, but at least she still had Ernest. Kathleen needed him to come home now, right that minute; she needed him to hold her, love her, and she was ready to receive it – in any form or fashion that Ernest wanted.

Ms. Fasse and Kathleen arrived at the apartment building, and parked her car in the space that coincided with her apartment number. The building was five stories high, and very clean. Everyone Kathleen had seen between the agency and the apartment seemed to wear shades. They had passed some noted beaches, and Ms. Fasse talked about "beach days" and how soon Kathleen needed to call the Minneola DMV about her driver's license. All of this sounded like a foreign language to Kathleen, and this must have been obvious to Mrs. Fasse, because she began to explain everything she had said. Preparing Minnie's future, Ms. Fasse continued, "Just as soon as you study a bit, we are going to the Department of Motor Vehicles in Minneola and get your driver's license. You do drive don't you?" Kathleen nodded her head. "Then you can drive and help do the marketing." That was another thing she needed to write down- northerners went to the market-not the grocery store. Even the person who took care of the apartment building was not the janitor, but "the super." "You are such a dear," Mrs. Fasse laughed. "Are you Italian?" Kathleen asked Ms. Fasse. "No, dear, we are Jewish. Oh, we're here already." Now, you are going to meet one of the most handsome men you have ever seen." Walking into the living room from the back of the apartment was a willowy young man, who, at a glance looked almost the slobbering image of a very young Jerry Lewis. There was another boy walking with him who looked to be the same age; Mrs. Fasse thanked him and gave him a $20 dollar bill as he was leaving. "Teddy, baby, this is Minnie." Kathleen extended her hand and said, "Hi there...you can shake my hand, it's clean." He extended his and Kathleen reached and shook it. She thought, maybe this was a Jewish or northern custom of them putting out their hand first before you do. "My husband's not home yet, Minnie, but let me show you to your room and the rest of the apartment. Teddy, take this for her, will you?" She picked up one of Kathleen's bags and gave it to Teddy. Kathleen noticed that Teddy seemed a little off-center, as if he was special, but on second thought, she tried not to stare at him. Something was different about this boy, how he looked at her and how he walked, but she could not pinpoint what it was. Mrs. Fasse continued with the tour. "I hope you like your room. It used to belong to our housekeeper, Emma Lee; she was with us 15 years, and she was a gem. Not a month ago Emma went home." Kathleen trying to be comforting said, "Oh, I'm sorry. Had she been ill? How did she die?" Teddy began to laugh and fell on the loveseat hide-a-bed that was to be Kathleen's saying, "She... she's not dead. Emma just went back to her hometown-to South Carolina. Kathleen sat her purse down near Teddy's feet and took a seat near him as he continued to laugh to explain how down south in "going home" meant dying, and that was why she misunderstood. Again she noticed his eyes being a little odd and a small scar between them. He was a handsome boy, but there was definitely something wrong with his eyes.

Mrs. Fasse chastised Teddy for laughing at Kathleen. She said, "Now, Teddy, it was not that funny; Minnie made an honest mistake. Let's let her get some rest, now. Minnie, I'll go over the schedule and the contract with you later. You're in luck, we're having Chinese for dinner tonight; is there anything special that you would like? "No, ma'am," she replied, "I don't know anybody from here but Dorothy. If you don't mind when the Chinese people come, I would like to stay in my room. I would rather not meet anybody else new until I can do my hair tonight, except for your husband, of course." This time, Ms. Fasse could not help bursting into laughter along with Teddy. Kathleen almost laughed, too, as the laughter was contagious, but she did not have a clue as to why they were cackling like chickens. Mrs. Fasse could hardly compose herself to speak- "Minnie, Minnie, Minnie! Honey, when I was talking….talking… a… about having Chinese for dinner, I meant that…. that we were having Chinese food for dinner, not people. You are so cute; I see now that you are going to be a source of great fun for my son. He hasn't laughed like this in years. Come on, Teddy, darling, let's give Minnie some privacy." Suddenly something happened that cleared Kathleen's curiosity about why Teddy got up from the loveseat and tripped over her purse. His voice was filled with fear as he screamed from the pain that he felt. Kathleen thought that he over reacted to the fall, as he reached frantically for somewhere or someone to get him up yelling. As Kathleen and Ms. Fasse began helping him, Teddy yelled, "Help me! Hurry Mother! Will you, help me; damn it!" Then he asked, "What was that, what was that, Mom?" Mrs. Fasse answered calmly, "It was Minnie's purse, dear; I'm so sorry, I'm so sorry. Are you all right? Then he angrily replied, "Hell no! You know you have to keep everything the same, I told you, I fucking told you that Mom!" He struggled to the door, walked out of the room, down the short hall to the right where his room was, and slammed the door. "What have I gotten myself into?"- Kathleen thought. Mrs. Fasse was clearly upset; she shook her head and rested her hand on Kathleen's shoulder in a reassuring manner and said, "He's alright, Minnie, it was not your fault. Ever since the accident, he gets scared if things are out of place. The world just seems a little difficult for Teddy right now, and he's a little embarrassed. You rest, now, and I'll see you in a couple of hours." Mrs. Fasse closed the door, and Kathleen picked up her purse and put it on the sofa. Pensively, she sat with an astonishing look and thought out loud, "Damn, the boy is blind."

Canned Heat (diary) was a mixture of rubbing alcohol and Kool-aid with water, boiled for some length of time before consumed.

CHAPTER II

One Hit

Kathleen anticipated meeting Mr. Fasse, thinking that he would be as nice as his wife was. Furthermore she hoped that he wouldn't have the slightest hint of anything that would remind Kathleen of men she had met back home. Kathleen knew how uncomfortable the working situation could become if the same were true of Mr. Fasse like some of the men in Memphis. As she rose from the sofa, Kathleen wondered about several things: What caused Teddy's blindness? Why did Emma leave, and why did Ms. Fasse choose her over Dorothy? Maybe, in time, Kathleen might have the answer, but the fear of Ms. Fasse discovering who she really was had already begun to gnaw at her. Dorothy had warned her, "You better forget telling the truth for once, girl, or you'll find yourself on the next bus back home or in the street." The guilt plus the hunger to see familiar faces was already growing, but Kathleen planned to resist the temptation to confess or leave. Although she did not know what her next move was going to be, Kathleen, alias Minnie, had better take advantage of this New York opportunity to change the direction of her life, because it might be her last one.

Kathleen was still tired from the bus ride, and the two hours were almost up before Mr. Fasse got there. She realized that she had to get adjusted to so much, the change in time, the North, Jews, and a blind boy who she would have to help take care of. She walked around, rubbed the tips of her fingers over the furniture, and smiled at the scenic room that was now hers. A real-live color television; something she had only seen in the homes where her grandmother worked, was in her room to turn on whenever she wanted. Mrs. Fasse must have heard her stirring around and knocked on her door. "Are you up Minnie? We're waiting for you, dear? She knocked while simultaneously opening the door. Kathleen combed her hair, washed her hands and followed Mrs. Fasse around the apartment for a tour. "Mr. Fasse is not home yet, but he will be here before six. Now, I have a list of things for you, and I do want to apologize for Teddy's outburst earlier. I hope you understand why. Did you rest well? Kathleen replied, "Yes, ma'am." Ms. Fasse explained, "You and Teddy will have to use the same bathroom, but Mr. Fasse and my bathroom is off limits except in an emergency." Minnie would never have to worry about cleaning it either, Mrs. Fasse added, because she liked doing that.

Kathleen looked at the antique dining room set and how Mrs. Fasse took pride in showing off the special china stored at the bottom of the cabinet and the family crystal on the top shelves. She beamed as she showed Minnie the cotton and silk china covers with zippers for the dishes to seal them from dirt or dust. The dining set was partially beveled and had ivory, with tiny gold trimming around it. A crystal chandelier that would take forever to clean hung over the center of the table.

Mrs. Fasse said that she bought fresh flowers every 3 or 4 days from Waulbaums, a market down the street and around the corner. They were center of the table and in memory of her mother, who she said loved to garden in the "old country." Kathleen wanted to cry at the mention of Mrs. Fasse's mother, because she had done nothing to pay homage to her own mother, and felt very guilty. The tour continued near the small kitchen and mirrored breakfast room, which had an oak table with the lever taken out, which sat on a marbled floor. "This is where the family eats breakfast at seven a.m. sharp, Minnie, "Mrs. Fasse said. After showing her the hall and closets, they walked to Teddy's room, which was closed. A KEEP OUT sign was on the front, with a small bell hanging from it. Mrs. Fasse shook the bell, and nothing happened. She shook it again, then the door opened and Teddy spoke. "No purses or suitcases allowed! Ladies, you may enter my domain, but do not bring any germs in here. I will have your heads if you cause my fish to die from that river of perfume you poured on. Welcome, while I give you the tour." This room brought a smile to Kathleen's face. This time she looked at Teddy and noticed how comfortable he was. He moved like a sighted person; everything was in place or rather had a place that even a new visitor would think of as a museum. There was no dust anywhere, but a rather large aquarium of exotic fish. Teddy introduced each by name as if he were looking right at them. There was a ham radio and high-fidelity set in the one corner, along with a collection of shells and souvenirs in another corner. The room was bright and cheery with a large mural of a tropical forest on one wall.

Teddy opened the closets and explained how he liked his clothes. Teddy put Kathleen to shame, she thought, because this boy's closets were immaculate. All shirts that were solid colored were together, while all printed ones were in another area. The shoes were set together with coordinated colored socks inside of them. Two pairs of sneakers were together, as well. Teddy's room and the rest of the house was a lesson in order, and Kathleen took note. She was impressed to see this, but wondered if she could live up to these folks' expectations. On her best day, Kathleen had never been that organized.

Teddy asked, "Can you make potato pancakes, Minnie? Emma could really make them." "No," Kathleen replied, "but if you show me how, Mrs. Fasse, I can do it. I can learn how to do anything," she added eagerly. But Mrs. Fasse did not know how to make them either. Instead, she took Kathleen into the kitchen and showed her cream cheese, locks, sturgeon and the staple of all Jewish breakfasts- bagels. She had never seen or heard of any of these except cream cheese. In all the old movies she watched and all of the old books she had read, Kathleen could not recall a bagel ever being mentioned. How did this escape her, she thought? Later on that day, Kathleen remembered a television show about a man named *The Great Gilderslieve*, and recalled the doughnut-like bread- a bagel. The fact that these people could eat fish in the morning was a shock to Kathleen. Mrs. Fasse demonstrated how to make the breakfast sandwich of sorts, reiterating that it was Mr. Fasse's routine breakfast. Ms. Fasse mentioned that Teddy would decide each morning what he wanted, and that Kathleen should make a list of what she liked. "Doesn't anybody eat bacon in New York?" she asked. Teddy and Ms. Fasse looked at each other and smiled. "When you're

Jewish, pork is not usually part of your diet." Now I must say, some Jews, including myself, have tasted bacon every once in a while, but it's something that most of my people do not eat. And if you're Orthodox, you don't come in contact with any forbidden foods or anything else that's not kosher or permitted."

Mrs Fasse asked, "You don't know anything about Jewish people, do you, dear?" Kathleen replied, "No, and I don't think that I have ever met any down home, but we have them, I know we do; I just don't know one." Ms. Fasse continued, "I would think that the agency would have informed you since New York, and especially Long Island is heavily populated with Jewish people. I think that Jewish people use their service more than anyone else's." Teddy brought up something that made Mrs. Fasse smile, "Do you know Sammy Davis Jr., Minnie?" "Yes, no, I mean, I know of him. But I've seen him on TV, why?" Teddy smiled and said, "Well, he's Jewish and he's colored- so you do know a Jew, Minnie."

Teddy had another laugh and stopped abruptly to go to the front door. Kathleen did not hear anything, but apparently Teddy was able to hear the key turn and his father turn the knob. "Sorry, sir, we don't want any," Teddy said. A very refined New York City accent resonated throughout the house, "Sorry sir, I don't have any. Give me a hug, will ya?" Teddy hugged his Daddy as if he had been gone for days. Kathleen was led down the hall to the living room to a short balding gray haired man, who wore a tailored dark blue suit. Kathleen was only 5'4", but Mr. Fasse was about an inch taller than she was. He extended his hand and greeted her, "Hello, there, young lady. I understand you have opted to stay with us and see if we will be the family that you want. I'm Jacob, but you can call me Jake or Mr. Fasse. Oh, and don't tell me, I am psychic- you are,… um, I know, don't tell me- you're Finnie? No uhm Hinnie? No, it's Minnie, right? 'Glad to have you aboard. It's about time Betty had someone to help her with this handful, referring to himself and Teddy. Now, if you will excuse me, I have to run to the little girl's room. Coming from a home with 4 sisters, I never heard it referred to as the little boys' room, so this is all I know. The guys at my office look at me funny when I say that." He laughed and said, "I'll be right back." Mr. Fasse moved quickly, taking off his suit coat and loosening his tie as he moved into the master bedroom.

Teddy quickly spoke, "That's Dad, Minnie, the bathroom king. No matter what time he comes home, he has to go to the bathroom, a conditional reflex. Well, what do you think of us, Minnie? Do we pass? Will you stay? Kathleen smiled and said, "Maybe, if you'll show me how to work that radio you have." The doorbell rang, and Teddy yelled, "I'll get it," as Kathleen observed how happy Teddy was for someone who was blind. She had 20/20 vision and hardly ever smiled.

Mrs. Fasse followed Teddy to the door and paid for the food. A very good-looking black man brought the order, and almost missed his tip staring at Kathleen. Men had always looked at her like that since about age 12, and she was used to it. Observing the stare from the delivery man, Mrs. Fasse quipped as she tipped him, "I have a lovely daughter-in-law, don't you think, young man? Too bad she's married or she probably would talk with you. Thank you." Teddy put his arm around Minnie as Mrs. Fasse closed the door. The look on the delivery boy's face when Teddy hugged Kathleen was extremely funny, and they all laughed.

47

Mr. Fasse returned and asked what all the laughter was about. Teddy said, "It's not every day my wife and I have time to talk to you, father. We've been going yachting around the world lately." Kathleen began to understand that these older parents adored their son, who was a jokester like his father. Again, Kathleen wondered where she could fit into all this, and how long she could continue to lie to this nice family about who she really was and why she was there.

Mr. Fasse and the family asked her to join them for dinner. Kathleen watched as Mrs. Fasse put place mats on the table and real plates instead of paper ones for the meal that had just been delivered. Intricately patterned glasses were set on the table and napkins for everyone. Mrs. Fasse showed their new maid Minnie where everything was, and asked her to sit with them for dinner. Kathleen was uncomfortable, but tried hard not to show it. Back home, Kathleen fancied herself at ease with white people, after all she had been around them all her life. Her grandmother saw to that every summer and school holiday, but breaking bread like a family member only happened when she was a little girl going to work with her Grandmother. This was the first time that Kathleen had eaten chow mien or used chopsticks. Teddy found it amusing to show her how to use them, even though he chose to eat non-combination foods. Kathleen learned that the thought of putting foods in his mouth like stews or mixed vegetables caused him to panic. He could eat sweet & sour chicken only if the pineapple was put in a separate bowl.

Kathleen always thought that being blind must be the worst thing in the world, but somehow Teddy made it seem uncomplicated; almost normal. After eating, Mrs. Fasse

48

showed her how to load up the dishwasher after seeing that Kathleen was about to wash the dishes in the sink, the way she had always done. Down home, her grandmother used the dishwasher on the job, but Kathleen knew of no one in her neighborhood who ever had one. "You can run the dishwasher every morning, Minnie and then put all the dishes away from the night," Mrs. Fasse told her. "That way Mr. Fasse doesn't have to hear the sound of appliances at night. He's a light sleeper, and gets crankier than an old T-model if he doesn't get his eight hours. We'll look at the schedule in the morning. Oh, but don't forget you will need to be up and in the kitchen by 6:30 or so to make the coffee. Better still, put four scoops in tonight and just turn the switch on in the morning. Now, let me see you smile before I go; I know you miss home, but this is your home now, dear."

Kathleen tried to sleep, but she kept seeing her grandmother each time she closed her eyes. She turned on the tiny gold-trimmed lamp, which set on the round table near the bed and thought about calling him. She had called him on the day before she left, hoping that he would stop her from going, but he hung up in her face after commenting with one word- "Really?" She picked up the receiver and listened to the hum for a moment. Just as she was about to dial, Kathleen changed her mind, turned off the light, and slid down under the covers with soft tears.

The morning came quickly, or so it seemed to Kathleen. She set the table, made the coffee, laid out the locks and bagels as Mrs. Fasse asked and went back to her room. After Mr. Fasse left for work, Kathleen began cleaning the kitchen. Mrs. Fasse watched how quickly Kathleen worked, and with such enthusiasm and speed as if someone had given her a deadline. Such action was ritualistic back home, for as soon the work was complete, the sooner Kathleen could look at whatever she wanted on her grandmother's television- a privilege her stepfather hardly ever allowed on the family's TV. If it wasn't sports or some shoot-em-up like *The Rifleman*, John Wayne, or Bonanza, little else was permitted for the children in the house to see. She anticipated watching the color television in her Long Island room, as Kathleen was an avid viewer of *The Edge of Night*, and *General Hospital*, which were her mother's favorite soap operas. Since little else could be enjoyed because of her mother's illness, watching television was one of few pastimes that she and her mother shared. In some strange way, this made Kathleen feel as if her mother was still with her.

Mrs. Fasse asked Kathleen to sit down in the living room, while she explained things that included the running of the household to Teddy's accident. One pressing item of interest was Kathleen's salary, and how much would be deducted from it each week. The contract that Kathleen signed stated that "a reasonable amount of money shall be deducted from the employee's salary until the amount for transportation and expenses of said employee are paid in full." Ms. Fasse would pay Kathleen $5 more, or $65 per week bi-weekly. Kathleen had never earned more than $45 a week, and $65 was great as far as she was concerned. The pay week would be on alternate Thursdays, in cash, until a checking or savings account could be established by the employee. Social security and other deductions would be made as designated. The two women went over the clauses concerning dismissal and conduct. Most of the contract was routinely written, but Mrs. Fasse was adamant about one subject-men. She did not want men in her home or calling their telephone late at night. Any long distance calls from Memphis would be okay, as long as she was informed. Some of Mrs. Fasse's friends had fallen prey to burglaries from unsavory characters associated with their help. There had even been one assault, which frightened Mrs. Fasse even more, so she warned Minnie to be aware that men, especially cab drivers, who might try to acquaint themselves. Mrs. Fasse got a phone call, and asked Minnie to wait for her.

The agency from Memphis and New York had a good thing going Kathleen thought: They could send women from the south to New York to cook and clean for rich people, collect an inflated fee for transportation and goodness knows what else. It was even more apparent that New Yorkers would pay well for a southern girl; as Mrs. Fasse hinted when talking about several of her friends using the same agency. A wise black girl from the north, who might have had more education, would probably not accept domestic work as readily as a southern one- but Kathleen could do little else. She was very observant of the immaculate way Mrs. Fasse kept the apartment, and she planned to do the same. Returning from her phone call, Mrs. Fasse gave a few more words of advice to Minnie about scheduling, while adding that she had great relief having hired her. Ever since Emma left, she and Mr. Fasse's life became stagnant, with little or no time for them to take a few days away without Teddy. Minnie, as Mrs. Fasse thought, was now going to provide their family with that luxury.

Her marketing day was usually every Thursday, so Mrs. Fasse thought that Minnie should go with her as soon as Teddy's best friend got there. Uniforms for Kathleen had to be purchased, and foods that she liked to eat, but she was warned that they were going into a Kosher supermarket.

When Teddy's friend, Bernie, got there, the ladies left, even though Kathleen had not finished her housework. Teddy kissed his mother goodbye, and went back to bed. It was chilly outside and Kathleen used her newly issued key to go back to the apartment to get her sweater. As she was leaving her room and passed Teddy's she heard him saying something about "ass" and Bernie laughing. Somehow, she just knew that they were talking about her, so she eavesdropped –hearing Teddy's voice- "I mean it, Bernie! I think that she might give me some of that colored cunt after she's here a couple of weeks. Are they really as big as grapefruits?" Bernie answered with a slurping sound, "Bigger, man, bigger; see if you can get her to lick my balls, man, 'cause she's got some luscious lips." Teddy jumped to Kathleen's defense immediately. "She's colored you fool, and I heard that they don't do that unless they're prostitutes." Kathleen tiptoed out and shut the door, running down the hall to the elevator. Should she tell Mrs. Fasse of the nasty little conversation she just heard; she wondered? No. Kathleen remembered what her grandmother told her about telling tales about blood only to blood- and check what you say to others; especially white people: either no one would believe it, or no one would care. When she got downstairs, Kathleen still contemplated telling Teddy's mother, but the voice of Dorothy rang like a bell in her head, "You better keep your big mouth shut, girl, with your honest ass, or you will be sorry." Mrs. Fasse had informed Minnie that she had more than one errand to run; then they would go to her sister's house. Kathleen would soon find out they had more in common with Mrs. Fasse's sister than she knew. Memphis lies and perceptions wandered through Kathleen's mind as Mrs. Fasse drove for a distance.

When Ernest got back to Memphis from the game, Kathleen told him how her uncle lied about her and Dorothy and her grandmother believed it. Kathleen struggled to tell Ernest about the incident and how embarrassing it was, when suddenly he told her that he, too, had heard that Dorothy went both ways. Ernest confessed that he even wondered if there was more than just friendship between her and Dorothy. Maybe that was why Kathleen was reluctant to have sex with him. Having sat close to him while they talked, Kathleen looked up at him in anger, snatched up her purse and proceeded to open the door of the white Chevy Impala when Ernest grabbed her arm. She was infuriated that he could think that, but when he began explaining, it all seemed logical. Ernest explained how he and Kathleen had been seeing each other for nearly a month, but they had not made love. "You tease me, girl, and I can't take that. I feel like I'm…I'm falling in love with you. You kiss me like a woman who knows more than she lets on." Little did Ernest know that most of her experience consisted of practice kissing on her hand, and observing how actors kissed on soap operas and in old movies was Kathleen's guide.

While Kathleen felt herself to be a strong-willed girl, she had always kept her hormones in check, because she wanted to please her mother more than anything anyone. Kathleen's mother had told her from a religious standpoint about not to having sex before marriage, but they had not talked about the actual act itself. Kathleen was preoccupied with her mother's illness, but her mother was dead, and what Ernest was gradually getting to her.

Ernest apologized for speculating about Kathleen and Dorothy. He even admitted that he walked on eggshells when he talked to Kathleen about sex. Little did he know that Kathleen could listen to him talk all night long; he made her feel things that seemed to come naturally. She was hoping that Ernest didn't notice how warm her body temperature was as the night progressed. Kathleen thought that she probably felt more excited than he did. His arousal level was just more obvious than hers.

This was the night that Ernest was to surprise Kathleen by teaching her how to drive. She had begged him to do so many times, and he had promised that he would, when she was ready, but the driving in the car was not the only thing on Ernest's mind. Wisdom, age, and experience were the weapons or gifts that Ernest possessed. At 23, he knew his way around women, and it was time to use what he knew to get what he wanted and what he wanted was to be inside of Kathleen.

Ernest told Kathleen that he had to do a favor for his brother, Steve, before the lesson was to begin. He was two years younger than Ernest, and Steve was very handsome and paper sack tan to Ernest's jet black skin. Steve smiled all the time, played sports, and could probably get any woman that he wanted. Steve, Kathleen soon learned, was definitely Ernest's favorite brother and a partner in brotherly crimes. Kathleen wrote in her ledger/diary that, "Steve was a girl magnet, and as wild as a Thanksgiving turkey running from slaughter."

This particular night, Ernest had driven Steve over to his girlfriend's house, whose mother just happened not to be home for the weekend. This was to be the first of many antics that Ernest helped his brother perform. Kathleen really liked Steve, but resented how he always happened to maneuver the time she and Ernest spent together to do whatever he wanted. While on the way to the girl's house, Steve related his interest in Dorothy and asked Kathleen to tell her how he felt. Kathleen replied, "But you have a girlfriend or two already, Steve. Why go after Dorothy?" She looked behind her in the back seat and found him pulling three condoms from his billfold and putting them in his shirt pocket. Steve answered after a second or two, "The more the merrier, I ain't married to nobody. A man's got to sow his wild oats, ain't that right bru'?" Steve then stretched his hand out for Ernest to give him five, but after one look at Kathleen, Ernest declined an answer or a gesture.

The conversation as they rode changed to sports between the two men. "I'm gon' run down that track until I reach the goal line, then I'm gonna cross over, man, and try to run the other way again," Steve explained. Ernest added, "It's mighty hard for me to do that, man, I guess I don't have the legs that you got, but I think if I try my one leg might outrun yours sooner that you think." This did not seem to make sense to Kathleen, but she stayed out of what appeared to be coded language. Kathleen did not know that they were talking about plans for her and another girl. Steve got out and wrote the phone number of the girl's house on a matchbook and gave it to Ernest. In the doorway was a pretty and young petite woman smiling. Steve waved goodbye and put his arm around her and went into the lovely brick house in the Whitehaven subdivision, where well-to-do Negroes lived, and where Kathleen wished she had lived too. Steve may have been a ladies' man, she thought, but at least the ladies have a home they could call their own.

Kathleen's self-esteem dropped as low as ever by this time. Instead to concentrating on being alone with Ernest,

Kathleen was suddenly engulfed in the reality of where she came from, who she was with, and how lucky she was that anybody wanted her. Maybe if her mother had lived, and maybe if someone in her family had wanted her she would not seem like a poor wandering misfit; that maybe she would have had a home to "receive company" like other girls. She tried to fight back the tears that were welling up in her big brown eyes until Ernest put his hand on her chin and turned her head around. Kathleen looked at him and he asked her what was wrong. Kathleen then slid over into his arms as tears streamed down her face.

Mrs. Fasse could not wait for her sister to meet Minnie. During the drive, she mentioned that she had thanked God for sending her someone who she could instantly trust and was like a lump of clay. She planned to mold Kathleen into a real New Yorker, if she got her way, so that she would stay with them for as long as Emma did or longer. Kathleen could not understand Mrs. Fasse's preoccupation with lengthy employment, but she knew that was not on the top of her agenda of life. She wanted to be a singer or an actress, like her mother wanted, and she was going to be a mother one day just like her mother had been.

When the car pulled into the driveway near a gate, Kathleen found herself looking at several brick edifices that were similar. The sign above the entrance was **Peaceful Twines**, as Kathleen noticed how quiet the neighborhood was so quiet and peaceful that only the amplified sounds of chirping birds could be heard- hence the name. People were riding bikes, sitting on benches under trees, and walking their dogs; most of the people seemed to be the same age-old and white- and smiled acknowledging Mrs. Fasse as she pushed the button on a speaker. Minnie's voice came on pushing a button to open the gate to let her in. They parked in a numbered space and walked to an apartment that had potted plants on each side of the door. Before the doorbell could be rung, a woman, who stood about four and a half feet, came to the door wearing some of the biggest, thickest glasses Kathleen had ever seen. She and Mrs. Fasse hugged as if they hadn't seen each other for years; surprisingly, Minnie hugged Kathleen in the same way chanting, "So this is Minnie. Minnie, Minnie!" It was apparent to Kathleen that the way Jewish people greeted each other was intense, as if this were their last time seeing the other person. However Kathleen became a part of this ritual made her very happy and very much accepted into the family.

The ladies were there about half an hour, when Minnie began a friendly interrogation. "So, why didn't you go to college, you certainly seem like a bright girl, doesn't she, Betty? I know that if I were single, and looked like you, Kathleen, I would travel every month and see the world before I settled down." "That's exactly what she did, Minnie. My sister went anywhere she wanted and she never settled down," Mrs. Fasse added. The sisters sounded like two tennis players volleying and serving each other when old Ms. Minnie said, "How could you say that, Betty, I married before you did, and stayed married for nearly 30 years, God rest his soul, my Charlie. Oh, there was no one like him. He didn't mind where I went or what I did, as long as I was happy. You want to know why, Minnie? Because he was such a whore...like an old tomcat, God rest his soul." Kathleen raised her eyebrows, choked on the soda and stood up with her mouth agape. She eventually put her hand over her mouth to stop the laughter. Minnie was a character, and a welcome change from the people Kathleen had just met. "Sit down, Dearie, I meant what I said. Charlie was a good provider; his diamond business paid off well, and he was a financial wizard who made great investments in business and insurance- and I would not have traded him for any other man in the world-except maybe Gregory Peck. Now there's a looker if ever there was one. Well, enough of that. I understand that you are wearing my name, young lady, and I might add that if we both walked down the street right now, I'm sure people would say that we're twins. Look at you. You have my young figure, my young looks and I have all the old wrinkles." Looking up Minnie added, "Oh, why did you give all the youth to the young?"

The ladies sat and talked for over an hour. While Kathleen understood that this was really a meeting to assess her, it was apparent how much Mrs. Fasse respected her sister's opinion. Kathleen began to feel like a first class con artist; she wanted desperately to unload the circumstances of the deception to them, but the voices of Dorothy and her grandmother had a more profound influence on her. Kathleen was not certain how long she would continue to keep quiet. By the time the sisters finished talking about their lives as children and bashing every old boyfriend they ever dated, nearly two hours passed. Mrs. Fasse looked at her watch, kissed her sister goodbye, old Minnie hugged young Minnie, and they left to go to the market; taking her sister's list of items to pick up. Kathleen felt comfortable enough to ask Ms. Fasse, "Did I pass your sister's test?" Mrs. Fasse laughed and answered, "With flying colors, my dear, with flying colors. They both laughed as they drove towards Waulbaum's Supermarket, back in Rockville Center.

Kathleen dried her tears with tissue from the box that Ernest kept in the car. She told him that she felt that she was not a girl from the right side of the tracks, or one he would be proud to bring home to his mother if she was still alive. She wanted Ernest to tell her if he was ashamed of her, whether it mattered where she came from, and if she had goals or an education. It was as if Kathleen expected rejection from him; any action that reminded her of the path her life had taken might be seen as unwelcome in a relationship. Kathleen didn't think that she wasn't worth much, so she didn't deserve much; especially not Ernest. He really had fallen in love with Kathleen, but Ernest was not unlike any other 23 year old man-he wanted to go to bed with her. From his heart came words that Ernest did not intend to say, but looking into Kathleen's deep brown eyes had a way of forcing the depths of a man's feelings to pour from his mouth. "I'm a country boy, baby, but I have spent most of my life in the city, gambling, drinking and running around, okay? I like women; that's no secret, and I like you. I like you a lot; you know that. That girl who you saw Steve with is a pretty nice girl, and Steve likes her better than any other girl he sees. Her family lives in that big house, because her grandfather left it to her parents when he died. Before that, they didn't have a pot to piss in and a window to throw it out, hardly. So don't go thinking that just because everybody has a new car or a big house it makes them somebody. I don't give a damn where you came from as long as you end up with me, aw' ite?" Kathleen smiled as he pecked her on the lips. "Now, it's time for the driving lesson."

The state line of Mississippi was nothing but dirt road for as far as one could see. Swinnea Road was not far from the state line, so Ernest drove Kathleen there on an empty lot and showed her how to apply brakes and ease up off the accelerator. She had a soft touch with the wheel and the pedals, and followed directions well. She was ecstatic when he took her on the express way and had her get off at the next exit. Deceleration, acceleration, lights, brakes, hazard lights-she was a fast learner, a "quick study"-as her high school teachers used to say; Ernest, too, was a pleased teacher. When he decided that the lesson was over, he asked what she wanted to do next or where she wanted to go. Kathleen quickly answered without thought, "Whatever and wherever you want, honey" "I can drive, can you believe it?" Kathleen apparently did not know to what she was answering. She assumed that he meant where were they were going to eat or sit and neck. She liked to go downtown to the cobblestones by the river, where they would get out of the car and look out at the barges and the legendary Memphis Queen steamboat. She had never been on a boat, but enjoyed the serenity of the river and the romantic setting for Ernest to embrace her. Maybe he'd drive to Lincoln Park and they could sit and look at the moon again; maybe this time they could go without the police creeping up behind them with a light and hoping to find them in the backseat of the car. She liked kissing him most of the time, as he knew just the right amount of tongue to give, always beginning and ending with kisses on her neck, clavicle, and ears. At times, he would bite her lip softly, and Kathleen liked it.

This time she really felt like getting into the back seat of the car, but being the good girl that she had been and having a genuine fear of the sex act kept her from engaging. Ernest asked, "Do you really mean what you're saying- I can go wherever I want?" She replied gleefully, "Yes, I mean it." With the speed of lightning, Ernest drove downtown to Second Street across from a popular radio station and into the driveway of an unlikely place. Kathleen seemed surprised, but allowed him to go inside while she sat in the car. She was wearing a yellow skirt and sleeveless matching top, and her long hair was piled up on her head in little curls. Before he left the car, Ernest kissed her on the cheek and hugged her as if to say, "Thank you." Suddenly Kathleen froze when she saw the neon sign flashing- **The Trumpet Motel.** Visions of the Eureka Motel, the night with Cherita and the blind date popped up like a jack in the box. It was all that she could think of. She could feel herself breathing heavily and balling her fist up in defense, as she thought about what Ernest was doing in the lobby of that motel. Other women were sitting in the cars that were parked on the lot; looking in mirrors, combing their hair, freshening up their lipstick, while waiting on their respective partners. They all looked cheap and tawdry to Kathleen, until she realized how she must have looked to them. They were all at the sleezy motel for the same reason-sex. Whatever that entailed-Kathleen was the new prime candidate about to join the ranks. Oh, how she wanted to run, but her legs would not carry her, and the distance to a new base for safety was probably too far to go.

Then Ernest pleaded, "Look, if we could just go in for a while and talk, that's all I will do, I promise I can't get my money back, and, it's a shame to let the room go to waste. We...we can watch television, listen to the radio and I won't touch you if you don't want me to. If you feel uncomfortable, then we'll leave, I mean it. I am not trying to hurt you." Within minutes, they walked the staircase to room 217. Ernest opened the door and threw the keys on the dresser, while Kathleen looked around and sat in the chair. He turned on the television to some show that Kathleen did not watch- but listened to. It seemed like a variety show like The Hollywood Palace. Ernest sat on the bed and stared at Kathleen then looked at the television for ten minutes or so. Suddenly he got up, walked around the bed and bent over to kiss Kathleen. "That's all you ever wanted with me in the first place, wasn't it? I didn't tell you that I wanted to come here! I ain't doing nothing!" Ernest stared at her, gave a loud sigh and dropped his in obvious disappointment. He then asked Kathleen, "Why did you say that I could go wherever I wanted then? You didn't really mean what you said? Look, I'm taking you home- this is it. I can't take this damn teasing anymore. You either act like a woman, or act like a little girl." Kathleen retaliated, "What'you mean, act like a woman? Just because I don't go to bed with you, I ain't a woman? Huh? Okay then, just take me home, and if this is it, then this is it!" She folded her arms, tightened her legs, poked out her mouth and breathed heavily. The room was silent for a minute, but what seemed a lot longer to Kathleen. Ernest faced the door then turned around toward Kathleen and spoke, "Look, baby, I want to be with you, I really do, but I ain't gonna force you. Ernest waited a moment and tried to kiss her, but she would not respond- sitting on her hands so as not to touch him. Kathleen was literally shaking; no matter what he tried, she resisted, ignoring him totally until Ernest said, "That's it, shit, fuck it. I'll take you home. He went outside to light a cigarette, because he knew she didn't like the smell of smoke. While outside, he noticed the tire had a slow leak, and a flat was inevitable. He shouted "damn" and prepared to fix it. "As soon as I change the tire, I'll take you back."

When Ernest returned, he went into the bathroom to wash the dirt from the tire off his hands. Just before closing the door he told Kathleen that he loved her, and said that he was sorry if he offended her. Kathleen remembered that on two occasions Ernest had taken her hand and put it on his private asking her to stroke it. This time, Ernest wanted more, and Kathleen knew that it would be over. While he was in the bathroom, Kathleen got up from the chair and looked in the mirror talking to her dead mother, "I'm sorry, Mama, I'm sorry." She peeled off her skirt and top, folded them neatly and put them in a chair. She had on a yellow bra and panties and looked at the side of her body and how flat her tummy was. She was afraid for him to see her naked. Kathleen listened to the water running in the bathroom, and found herself staring at the bed. She took a big swallow, got in the bed, covered herself up to her neck with the sheet, and closed her eyes, tightly. The water stopped and Ernest entered the bedroom. Her eyes were still closed when Ernest said softly, "Open your eyes...are you sure?" She opened her tear-filled eyes and nodded-staring into his. He smiled, turned off the television, walked over to the dresser, and found a soft music station on the clock radio. Kathleen followed him with her eyes as he turned off the light switch and locked the door. Ernest undid his zipper while reassuring Kathleen in a very soft tone, "I promise that I won't hurt you, baby, I promise." Kathleen closed her eyes again; not knowing that this was the first of many more lies to come.

Living on Long Island and going to Waulbaum's was an event. Everyone who worked in the supermarket seemed to know Mrs. Fasse personally, and almost everyone shopping there stopped to talk with her. They would ask about Teddy or if Kathleen was their new "girl." How much like the south that conversation seemed, Kathleen thought, for no one could be anyone's woman, housekeeper or maid. But just as Mrs. Fasse was asked the "girl" question, she gave an unexpected answer, "No, she's our new housekeeper. Didn't you know that, 'girl' went out with high button shoes?" It was hard not to like Mrs. Fasse, no matter how Kathleen tried not to. She began, since day one, to act as a protector or a mother- figure for Kathleen, who was still a little wary of trusting Mrs. Fasse completely. Indoctrinated skepticism about white people could not be erased in Kathleen's mind in a few days or weeks. Kathleen was introduced to the butcher, and the store managers, the delicatessen workers, while getting approval for her to charge whenever she began her marketing chores. Kathleen thought about the things that she could get in the store without anyone telling her she did not have enough money. A sense of privilege came over Kathleen, as she felt respected, and even though she was only the Fasse's housekeeper.

After an evening of shopping for groceries and picking up two white uniforms for Kathleen to wear, Mrs. Fasse was exhausted. Teddy and his friend Bernie were on the Ham radio, and continued to do so, while Kathleen finished her chores. She began to make spaghetti with the marinara sauce and no meat, just the way Mrs. Fasse wanted it. A green salad with carrots diced and put on the side was arranged in the refrigerator, while she made a plain meatloaf. Teddy did not want anything on it except ketchup otherwise they would have had to throw it away. At dinner, when Mr. Fasse arrived, Kathleen sat all the food on the table and went to her room. After dinner, Mrs. Fasse came to her room and asked to talk with her about a matter of importance. "Minnie, have you ever served dinner to a family before now, dear?" Kathleen replied, "Yes, ma'am, did I do something wrong?" Mrs. Fasse's next continued without answering, "How did you serve dinner when you were in Memphis?" Kathleen was nervous by now, knowing that she had done something maids or housekeepers from New York did not do. "I...I just put everything on the table and left. See back home, I didn't work during dinner; I just kind 'a left it on the stove, and when they got home they would warm it up, I guess. Then they...they served themselves. I...I only served two parties and that was in a Doctor's fraternity house during Christmas and New Year's. I just walked around with a tray and kept getting new ones when they got empty. What did I do wrong, Mrs. Fasse?" She took Kathleen's hand and asked her, "You've never really worked as a live-in housekeeper, have you?" Kathleen replied, "No, ma'am, I haven't, but I never said that I did, why?" By this time, Kathleen was frowning and upset, seeing the look of disappointment in Mrs. Fasse's eyes. "Dear," she very kindly began, "according to the contract, you had been a live-in maid for a year or so for some prominent Memphians who lost you when they moved to another town. It stated that you didn't want to go with them and your signature is on the line where the statement is. "What statement, Mrs. Fasse? I didn't write any statement, neither of us did. I never wrote anything...wait a minute, when we got here, the lady had us to sign, but Dorothy and

I didn't read…what did we sign?" Kathleen began to panic, but Mrs. Fasse calmed her down. "Minnie, honey, it's alright. Mr. Fasse and I suspected as much. Some of these agencies bring young women here and well, for a better word, it is slavery." Kathleen stood up at hearing this, "That's against the law, Mrs. Fasse. Cain't nobody own nobody no more! What is wrong with you people? I knew it was too good to be true." Kathleen began to open the dresser drawers and get her clothes. "Wait, wait a minute, Minnie. There's no slavery here either; what I meant was agencies sometimes tell their clients that their employees have had a certain amount of experience and we, as clients are expected to believe them, because we are so in need of help, and they know it. I bought what they said, dear, not bought you. Now, look, if you will be patient with me, and I with you, I will teach you the things that you don't know about serving dinner, all right? Why don't we put the dishes in the dishwasher and talk about it. Don't fret. Some of my friends told me that the same thing happened to them."

Kathleen not only felt dumb, but very vulnerable. All the things her grandmother had taught her about trusting people left her when she signed that contract. She could have signed away her life. She wanted to tell Mrs. Fasse then and there how old she really was and who she really was, but now was not the time. It was like she was on base and it was crowded with other runners. The well of deception was becoming fuller each day and would soon run over. That evening, Kathleen got a quick lesson in how to serve dinner. She had not completely lied. Back home, they usually put everything on the table-bread, meat and vegetables, and they all ate.

Few times were salads served; that was something that was made with onions and beets whenever the great-uncles from Chicago came to visit. Her family could just afford meat and potatoes, let alone salad.

When Kathleen retired for the night, she took a piece of paper and copied the information that Mrs. Fasse gave her. Then she thought about the circumstances that brought her grandmother from Mississippi to Memphis, and how important a signature was in determining her family's fate. Kathleen recalled a story that she wrote in one of her ledger/diaries that her grandmother had told her: I had been working for this white family, the Fitch's, ever since I was nine years old- that was around 19 and 15 (1915). In school, I got as far as the third reader, when Mama and Papa took me out to help the family. I was the oldest girl, so they pretty much expected me to do that. Mrs. Fitch was a nice old white lady who asked for me to stay at her house, but I would come home on weekends. I made 50 cents a day, and her son would pay me every week. Most of the time, Mrs. Fitch would slip me a little more on the side, because she wanted to help my family, and I really liked her for doing that. I worked for her nearly four years, when Mrs. Fitch up and died one night from a bad heart. When the lawyer told me I was supposed to be at the Will reading, I found out that Mrs. Fitch left me her house that she lived in and three acres of land. Now these white folk owned most of the town, and didn't want for nothing. Her son came to the house not long after, and asked me if I wanted to sell it; said he would give me $500. Well that land was worth way more than that, Papa said, so I said "no." He came back a couple of more times, but he never went over $1000. My Papa and all of us packed up and got ready to move in, when the night before there was a hard, loud knock at the door. Papa opened it and three men came in with guns in their hands. One put a pistol to my Papa's head, while another one, who sounded a whole lot like young Mr. Fitch's voice told me to sign the paper. O therwise Papa's head would be on the floor. Then they left after almost knocking Papa out with they' pistol. We moved the very next day to Memphis- in Germantown, where a lot of sharecropping was going on. My Grandmother told me, "Don't 'never sign nothing child, if you can help it, unless you read it or somebody puts a gun to your head and makes you. You could be signing away more than you know." Some memories could not be written down; Kathleen could only close her eyes before bedtime and relive them.

Kathleen closed her eyes and tried to sleep; two things she did not want to think about, her carelessness in signing the work contract or thinking about and missing Ernest. She could get through the day and not think about him as long as she stayed busy, but it was the nights that were the hardest. The few nights that she had lain in bed with him, Ernest insisted that they spend the night together, and she almost always complied. She wanted to forget him, even though she ached to be with him; in the wee hours of the night under the covers, she sobbed- as she felt like a shipwrecked passenger on a deserted island. Kathleen knew that she was destined to cry herself to sleep many nights. She couldn't escape seeing every line in his face when she closed her eyes. Kathleen hoped that one day she wouldn't have to think about their time together and that maybe someone would come and rescue her from these haunting recollections. It was then that she learned and accepted masturbation. Although it made Kathleen feel very guilty, it also became her only relief when she thought of him. In her ledger/diary, Kathleen vowed, "I have to get over him. He's like a foul ball-you don't want to keep hitting them, because it stops you from getting a home run."

The apartment was empty except for Kathleen, and three days had passed since she became a "member" of the Fasse family. They had gone out for a beach day and Kathleen had decided to write a letter to her grandmother and let her know where she was. The phone rang with a very familiar voice on the other end. This was the first time that Kathleen answered the phone; she did so in a well rehearsed manner "Hello, Fasse resident?" The caller said, "Hey, girl, I guess our week is up." Kathleen shouted, "Dorothy! Girl, hey, how...how did you get this number, the week's not up yet?" Dorothy continued, "It's a long story, girl, but basically I told these people I was a member of the NAACP, and I was going to call the New York branch for maids that need help. Kathleen laughed, "And they believed you?" "Child, white folks will believe anything about colored people when you start throwing big initials around like the N double A CP., something they know nothing about." They both laughed, and arranged to meet on their mutual off day- Thursday. Kathleen planned to go to Dorothy's, because she wanted to see more of New York. Dorothy was on Long Island too, but more near the real suburbs, where each home had a swimming pool or was two to three-stories high. Dorothy told her that she lived near Betsy Palmer the game show queen of television's *What's My Line?* or other shows like it. Kathleen wanted to see where she lived; perhaps she might even get a glimpse of her. She had never seen a real television personality or movie star, and this seemed to be the closest opportunity to meeting one

69

or the other. Dorothy's employers were rich with inherited money, but were a little freaky.

Kathleen was going to take the bus to a point where she would get off, and then Dorothy would meet her. Dorothy was more familiar with the area having lived there on Long Island from her previous job at the *ABC Maid Agency*. Kathleen was amazed at Dorothy's resourcefulness. When she wanted to get away from Memphis the first time, she looked at an ad in the paper that said, "If you want to go to New York and see the world contact *The ABC Maid Agency*. Dorothy was gone for nearly six months, but she came back when her mother was ill. She had saved up at least $1000 to help her family. With the incident at the restaurant and being broke, the only chance for Kathleen and her to get away seemed to be the agency- and she took it.

When Mrs. Fasse and the rest of the family arrived, Kathleen told her about talking with Dorothy. Mrs. Fasse was amazed that they could find each other before the week was up, but Kathleen explained the persistence of Dorothy. Mrs. Fasse warned Kathleen about cab drivers and other men who might want to talk with her; she wanted her to be extra careful. She even suggested that Kathleen act as if she was mentally challenged in public, hoping that people would take notice and help her if need be. Kathleen thought that this was kind of funny and caring of Mrs. Fasse, but assured her since she traveled safely from Memphis to New York, she could handle herself quite well. Kathleen got the directions from Dorothy, and when Thursday came around Kathleen finished her chores and left around nine in the morning for the bus stop, as the Fasse's slept. While standing reading the directions, she saw a black car out of her peripheral vision, and it was Mrs. Fasse. Kathleen tried to ignore her, so she turned away from her. At first she became a bit angry, but realized that Mrs. Fasse cared about what happened to her, something Kathleen had not experienced for a long time. She smiled and got on the bus when it came. She watched Mrs. Fasse as the bus pulled off, and thought about her decision to come to New York. It felt good to have someone watching out for her interest- or, was she really watching out for her own-her housekeeper? Kathleen had now become like a family member, an object of concern, and she liked that feeling of importance. Her mind wandered to Memphis. Did Ernest ever really feel anything for her, or did he just want to get her into his bed?

It was dark in the room, and only moonlight shined through the window of Memphis' Trumpet Motel. Kathleen thought, "Why was it named that? Was it because whatever happened there would be like winning a war; like a victory sound; was she the millionth woman who lost her virginity there? Would she be different; would it hurt? Ernest eased down into the bed and under the covers, pulling her close to him. He began to kiss her, as he always did, but this time his breathing was heavier. The yellow bra, panties and half-slip that Kathleen wore were being taken off quickly, and he moaned with every move that he made-biting her neck and licking and biting her ear. His hands seemed rough and he needed lotion, she thought, as he touched her delicate skin. He seemed very intent on pulling her legs open. Why was he sucking her breast; is that what men did to women? It felt good as her nipples hardened, but then her light browned nipples began to hurt as he bit them and sucked

71

harder. Kathleen wondered why he was taking off all of her clothes, because surely he could do whatever he wanted just by removing the panties, or so she thought, without taking off all of her clothes or opening her legs. The truth was Kathleen didn't know what the sex act actually entailed. As had a good that "good funny feeling" in the bathtub, ever since she was fifteen, and never opened her legs. She simply rubbed her vulva repeatedly, closed her eyes and it happened. When Ernest took her panties off, she said "No" very softly, but there was no turning back now. This huge, long and thick thing was stabbing her leg and eventually invaded her-and it hurt badly! Kathleen screamed, but he kept on pushing it in. Tears were rolling down the side of her cheek. He began to bounce or hump for what seemed like an eternity; then he fell on her moaning and shaking like a mad man and biting or sucking her neck and breasts. He would not get up, and that horrible thing would not leave her body. It felt like a huge submarine had dropped inside her. Ernest fell into a deep sleep, but she did not, she could not. A sick feeling came over her, but she still did not move, thinking that he would be disappointed if she did. At that moment she hated him, she hated herself and every man that she ever met. She especially hated her stepfather for she finally knew what he had been doing to her mother before cancer made her very ill. She hated the greasy garage and the nasty old men at the corner. They had whistled at her since fifth grade; she hated the cars that passed with men yelling things out of the window to her. She hated all the boys who she had smacked upside their head, because they always wanted to hold her tightly during the school sock hops.

"Manish" as her grandmother would say, was what they were. She remembered how one a relative had copped a feel a few times in her sleep. She was around eleven and soon told her mother, but blamed herself for his being beaten half to death with an extension cord because of it.

Kathleen turned away from Ernest and cried. She cried for all women who ever endured this pain, and planned never to do it again, no matter what. My goodness, she thought, this is what Jimmy Lee wanted to do to her with that enormous bulge in his pants? She wanted to run, but her legs were weak, Ernest was heavy, and she could not move him no matter how hard she tried. At that moment, Ernest joined the ranks of other non-caring people Kathleen had met. She wondered, was it true that Ernest didn't care about her feelings? Was getting her into bed all that he wanted? All she wanted was for him to get up off her so she could throw up- because what he did had made her sick.

About 15 minutes or so later Ernest awoke and slid to the other side of the bed. Kathleen got up to go to the bathroom, feeling as if a Mack truck had run through her body. She looked down at the pool of blood on the bed, and went into shock. She opened her mouth and shook her head, but couldn't speak. While she covered it with the top sheet and chenille spread, she suddenly screamed so loudly from the blood running down her leg that the telephone rang from the management asking if they were fighting, or what, but Kathleen put her hand over her mouth as Ernest told the man on the phone that she had seen a spider and he killed it. Ernest asked, "What is the matter, baby?" Hysterically she cried, "I'm...I'm bleeding to death, I'm dying... take me to the hospital!" She shook uncontrollably as he tried to calm her down. He attempted to explain why this happened, and asked her not to panic. She ran into the bathroom, washed up, and when she returned she asked to be taken home. Ernest asked her to stay the night; it was already after one o'clock and he thought it would be convenient for him to leave from the motel and pick up Steve in the morning. Kathleen knew that this was the first clue to his insensitivity about her needs; that her feelings did not matter-but she pushed it back in her mind. Now, Ernest, of course, would now have to do something else to prove that he really loved her-after all, she reasoned, he had seen her naked and taken her virginity. He had made his hit-passed first base; now he would have to go to the next base, or so Kathleen thought. Of course, she didn't realize he had hit a home run, and she would be left on base to walk to the dugout-defeated, alone, and with another error.

When the bus stopped in Jamaica Plains, Kathleen knew that she had gone too far. She showed the bus driver her directions, the address, and he told her what bus to get on. After getting back on track, Kathleen ended up at her destination. Dorothy met her and they went back to what could be called nothing else short of a mansion. It was huge, with one of those drooping down looking like someone is crying trees in the yard that her grandmother called Weeping Willows. She went in the front door, something no southern employer would allow, and was met by a black curly male poodle, that was overly friendly.

Dorothy had maneuvered her employers into using the swimming pool all day, if she wanted to do so. They even supplied the swimsuits for the two of them. A very svelte long-haired blonde woman over forty was walking around wearing a silk pink peignoir with a cup and saucer in hand. She was headed toward the staircase, which split into two separate ways of reaching the landing. The hall was adorned with family photos; as Kathleen peeped into the living room, she saw Renaissance paintings on three walls and a huge fireplace. The woman spoke with a deep low voice, and she kept pulling her hair back from her face as she sipped her coffee. "Hello there, young lady, you must be Katy, right? I'm Lydia, Lydia Shaeffer. I know something about you. You don't like to be called Minnie, so you use your middle name. See, I remembered, didn't I Dorothy? Well you make yourself at home, honey. My husband may be walking around here half nude, but don't mind him, please. If there is anything that we can get you, that's not in one of the freezers, let us know. Oh, Dorothy, please, let the dog out for me; I know it's your off day, but Poopsy has become quite taken with you. Ciao." Dorothy gestured with her finger that the woman drank, then she answered, "Yes, Mrs. Schaffer, I'll be glad to." Dorothy did not particularly like dogs, but for the job, she could put up with anything. Dorothy had Kathleen follow her to the back door, where she let Poopsy out. The whole area was enclosed with an unusually high wrought iron and brick fence, so the dog could roam safely, and as Dorothy suggested, curious eyes could not see.

Dorothy whispered that there was "stuff" going on in the mansion. Kathleen sensed that she could hardly wait to tell her about it. She got two glasses of orange juice and was on her way out the back door, when a tall, plump, slightly balding man jumped from another room and yelled "Boo." This man's accent sounded like the actor Walter Slezak, who was the character *Macoco* in the Gene Kelly/Judy Garland movie *The Pirate*. Kathleen thought that he must be German, Austrian, or some sort of European immigrant. He did not hesitate holding her arm and saying, "Well, now, this must be Minnie, who you are always talking about, eh, Dorothy? You did not do her justice in your description on her. She's beautiful, stunning, if I may say so myself-and I do. Fredrick Shaeffer or Dr. Shaeffer to most," he said as he extended his hand. "Do you miss slopping the hogs and eating grits and fatback now that you're here in New York?" He laughed and added, "I was just kidding, just kidding." Kathleen immediately felt the blood rushing to her head and countered referring to the *Books of Knowledge* and *Reader's Digest* that she had read, "Probably not any more than people who baked and cooked people in the oven over there in Germany. I heard that they were still looking for war criminals- do you know any? Dr. Shaeffer slowly turned his grin into a frown, then Kathleen toned down her sarcasm with, "Just kidding, Dr. Shaeffer. It always upsets me when people think that Memphis is a country town. I was born in Memphis, 'never slopped a hog, but I have eaten smoked bacon, side meat, and grits. I think everybody up north believes Memphis is like the Beverly Hillbillies, but it's not, Dr. Shaeffer." Obviously impressed with the way Kathleen responded, Dr. Shaeffer added, "I was just kidding myself. I must say that I never saw any loose poultry flying around or any hens laying eggs. Dr. Shaeffer laughed at his own joke, but no one else did. Why don't you both come and sit down with me and have a bagel or an omelet? That juice is certainly not enough to start your day. Now listen to me, I am a physician, and I know best. Dorothy looked at Kathleen and gestured for them to sit. "Now, tell me, young lady, what are your plans? Have you given us a plus on the scorecard yet? Don't make a hasty decision based on the first impression of that "boo" that I gave you, and I do truly apologize for the inference to farm life. I can see that your lovely hands and tell that they have not been roughened by any farm work. He kissed one of them, but Kathleen did not pull away, trying to give the impression that she was used to this. She added, "I apologize too, but I get kind of angry when people think that all southerners are dumb." The doctor quickly changed that subject, "Now then, young lady, answer my question, please, what are your plans?" Kathleen looked at Dorothy and realized that it was time to take control of the conversation, for the Dr. was obviously flirting. Kathleen declared, "One day, I plan to be on Broadway." There was silence in the room, and as she saw the expression on their faces; "then I'll go back home a star, and buy the town." The doctor began to gradually laugh, which became louder and he added, "I think that you just might do that, little lady, you just might. After all, isn't that what that hip-shaking Elvis did? He became a star. Go and enjoy the pool. Be prepared to have your photo taken later. I'm really quite handy with the camera; you'll see. This is my day off, and I'm going to enjoy it." The doctor walked outside and played with the dog, leaving the ladies to their own devices. Dorothy could not wait to say something, "Whew, glad he's gone, he gets on my damn nerves, always flirting and going on with his old ass. But he sho' does like you, though. Have you ever seen such a big house in your whole life? And my room is on the third floor. Come on upstairs and I'll show you some stuff."

The girls drank the juice climbed the finely chiseled stairs to the third floor. Dorothy shut the door and they sat down on a day bed to talk about the Shaeffers, their open marriage, and how they travel to out of the way places. "They asked me the next day after I got here if I knew anything about swinging. Well, that's when they compared me to the Beverly Hillbillies. I told them that everybody I grew up with could swing, so what did that have to do with my job? Hmph, swinging, to them was different from what you and I know. Kathleen looked puzzled, so Dorothy explained, "Sleeping with as many people as they want, anytime, anyplace, and anywhere, girl, as long as they tell each other about it. Bullshit! I told them that I was here to work, and whether they swing or not ain't none of my business. They laughed at me, but I made myself damn clear." Kathleen's mouth was open until Dorothy went to another subject. Aw, girl, I called Lee the other day, and he said that he was going to leave his wife, that he missed me, and then he asked when was I gon' be coming home." Kathleen had heard the enthusiasm in Dorothy's voice before, only to see tears of sadness later on; so she quickly responded to this news, "Of course you told him that you were not coming home, right... right?" Dorothy hesitated and asked, "You don't want me to lie, do you?" Kathleen was livid, "Girl, you have talked me into coming all the way up here to change my life and the minute you here this niggah's voice you all ready to zoom back to Memphis!? Well, you go right ahead on, but I'm not going anywhere. I had enough heartache this past year to last me a lifetime. There's nothing back there- and nobody- well, maybe that's not true for you-your mother is still living." Kathleen walked toward the door to leave when she stopped her. Shug explained that she was not going anywhere now, but she still loved him. Lee had been the only man who she said "snapped her crackle and made it pop." Dorothy was always using some kind of euphemism about sex and usually equating it with food. Her life was predicated on sex, and little else interested her except money. Even though Kathleen listened to her declare what she would have no parts of; she even suspected that for the right price, Dorothy might give in to anything, even swinging.

Dorothy had an enormous amount of work to do in that mansion compared to what Kathleen had to do in the Fasse's apartment. Dorothy took her further up the stairs to the attic where there were numerous after-five dresses, designer clothes with dates from 1956 to the present tagged on them. Names like Cassini, Head, Chanel, Givenchy, were inside of them. Kathleen figured that Ms. Shaeffer could hardly wear the same dress twice, as Dorothy showed her old articles and photos from society news and the charity events she had attended. The guests were dressed like kings and queens, famous actors, political figures standing or sitting near Ms. Shaeffer, who wore expensive looking jewels from her head to her wrist. Kathleen began to envy Dorothy a little, as she thought of the exciting parties that she would serve where movie stars and politicians might gather. All Kathleen had to look forward to was Teddy and his friend Beenie suffering from teenage hormones and a filthy mouth. Dorothy mentioned that the Shaeffers told her of previous parties; others they were going to have in the near future, and that they might need extra staff to help serve. "Oh, please, get me, ask me, girl! I'll do it. If it's after dinner, my time is my own," Kathleen pleaded. Dorothy assured her that she would.

The latter part of Kathleen's visit was spent walking around the grounds.

They finally went to the bathhouse, rinsed off and got into the bathing suits. Mrs. Shaeffer had gone shopping and told the girls that the house was theirs. Kathleen had begun to have a suspicious mind about a woman leaving her husband home with two young women, so she hesitated putting on her bathing suit. She thought that she saw an eyeball through a hole in the bathhouse wall, but after looking again, she chalked it up to her imagination. The girls walked out to the pool and stepped into an area that covered about four feet of water. Kathleen was afraid of deep water, and remained in the four feet, while Dorothy went toward the ten-foot area. She beckoned for Kathleen to follow her, but she wouldn't go. Instead, she looked behind her and saw Mr. Shaeffer near the bathhouse in his big old baggy trunks snapping pictures. She realized then the eyeball she thought that she saw was his and his watching them undress and slip into the swimsuit may now become a snapshot for his old man memoirs. Kathleen got out of the pool, wrapped herself in a towel, and sat on the lounger. She decided to do something she always knew that she had in her, but used sparingly-she began to tease the old man. She lifted her right leg in the air and dried off with the towel, slowly, then the left leg. She got up and straightened the flowered bikini bottom and got back on the lounger. Mr. Shaeffer could not stand it any longer. He walked over and asked if he could take some pictures of Kathleen and she complied. He said that he did not want poses, just natural action- no looking at the camera. He was red as a beet and breathing like a snorting pig; by this time, Dorothy had walked over and began posing anyway. Shug seemed oblivious to the strands of pubic hair that crept from under the bikini bottom she wore, but knowing her as Kathleen did, Shug probably thought that look to be attractive. Back home, hairy-legged females was not uncommon with teachers as most black women did not shave their legs. Kathleen, on the other hand, after watching years of the cosmetic routines and habits of white women in the movies- especially the movie *Some Like It Hot*- shaved all the hair on her legs and other areas after seeing some of the nasty books that were under the mattress of a family her grandmother had worked for. Only a small line or patch was in the middle, but elsewhere, there was no hair. Besides, Kathleen could never recall seeing Esther Williams with hair around her bathing suit.

Shug was enjoying the camera, but when Dr. Shaeffer stopped, he offered a proposition. "I pride myself on being a good photographer, ladies, and I have won a few contests. Why don't we go inside to my little studio and I'll show you?" They followed him to a door not far from the kitchen where a larger camera on a swiveling tripod stood. A mural of a beach scene, a towel and beach ball were fixed on the wall that the camera faced. He closed the door quietly and turned on brighter lights on the beach scene. "Why don't you girls take off your tops, sit on the towel, and I'll tell you how I want you to pose?" Kathleen raised her eyebrows and put her hand on her hip in the fashion reminiscent of her grandmother and told him, "I'm not taking off anything; I don't mind taking a picture, but I am not taking off my top. Dorothy followed suit with, "Me neither."

Dr. Shaeffer, seeing how angry he was making Kathleen, asked that the girls just sit on the towel and take the picture as they were. Dorothy has a swimming cap on over her long human hair wig and did not want to take it off. Kathleen had her curly hair pinned up in a ball. She took it down and shook it, sat on the towel and posed as Dr. Shaeffer asked.

81

After several poses, he asked the girls to hold each other and place their legs in certain positions that seemed quite sexual in nature. Kathleen threw her hand up and shook her head, indicating that she was not complying with any such request. Then Dr. Shaeffer offered to pay the girls $50 each to pose, then $75 and eventually $100. Dorothy's eyes opened wider at the prospect of making fast money and looked at Kathleen, then quickly excused herself and took Kathleen outside of the studio. "Look, girl, for that much money, we could pretend anything. He is just an old freak trying to have some fun. Come on, hear?" Kathleen replied, "You so quick to do anything; do you remember all the stuff you said about trusting people? Do you want some old dirty picture floating around of you when you get old and have grandchildren? He better go and get himself a prostitute or something, cause I ain't giving up nothing, showing nothing or taking no more pictures. Look, let me use the phone so I can find out how early the bus runs- I'm ready to go home. Dorothy knew that Kathleen meant business, so she went back in and told Dr. Shaeffer no for the both of them. Kathleen was on her way to the bathhouse to rinse off, dress and leave. She figured that Dorothy would probably take Dr. Shaeffer up on the proposition eventually, but she was having no part of it. When she got back inside the house she called the bus station, got the information, and found that the bus would be leaving in a little more than an hour. Dorothy apologized for asking her, and they went back upstairs to her room. Within minutes there was a knock at the door; it was Mrs. Shaeffer, who apparently was never really gone as they thought. "Girls, I don't know why you turned down the money, but the next time he offers make him pay twice as much. He's really a good photographer. When he finishes, he paints nudes and sells them. Oh, Dorothy, I have a few things laid out in the closet for you to look at. Kathleen may want two or three of them. You are more than welcome to them; I won't be wearing those anymore. You come back soon, Kathleen, and maybe my husband won't be so rude the next time. Ciao."

How did Mrs. Shaeffer know what happened, the girls wondered? Dorothy started to talk about what had just happened, when Kathleen put her hand over her mouth. She whispered that they would talk when they got outside. Mr. Shaeffer waved goodbye to Kathleen as she was leaving, and Dorothy walked her to the bus stop. "Look, Shug, those people you work for may be rich, but you better watch out. They have intercoms in almost every room, and there is no telling what else. You'd better be careful and not let them put you in a trick. How much do you have to pay them back for the trip?" Dorothy did not want to talk about it, but Kathleen kept asking her. "They told me if I worked on my off days they would not take out much. They pay weekly up here, but I told them to pay me every two weeks; I make $60 a week." Kathleen told her that that was $10 a day, and not to give up any off day. "Tell them that you want to pay $5 per week, that's all. These people are real funny acting, and doing some weird stuff. You better watch out, and don't trust anybody- that's what you told me; remember? Look, we'll talk. Stay away from that man and watch that woman; she looks kind of strange to me. Anyway, thanks for the dresses." Dorothy hugged her goodbye when they saw the bus coming and ran back to the mansion. When Kathleen got settled on the bus, she looked back at the mansion and realized how lucky she was to be working for the Fasse family. They may have had a blind son and a smaller place, but Kathleen was content that there was nothing weird about them; not like the Shaeffers. As Kathleen looked around the bus, she noticed how the people seemed to look at her. She wondered if she had that "I'm not from here look." Having boasted about her ability to mock people, Kathleen decided that she was going to adopt the accent of New Yorkers. Since childhood, she had been able to absorb dialects and accents whenever she chose; this was an opportunity to sound like a real New Yorker. Anything to get the sound of the south from her lips-the sound of Memphis- and what she had done to not be a "good girl" anymore. Kathleen's mind wandered back to Memphis, and continued throughout the long bus ride back to the Fasse's.

The next morning, Kathleen arrived home around seven. Ernest could not take his hands off her as he helped her to the door. He had wanted to pick up Steve, but Kathleen urged him not to until he took her home, because she did not want Steve to know that they had spent the night together. He kissed her on her forehead, and said that he would call her. She went in and could not sleep for several reasons- the pain she was experiencing and the way Dorothy's grandmother was looking at her when she arrived in the morning. Either she was a dumb old lady, or she was wise enough to say nothing about the time of day Kathleen arrived. Surprisingly, she opened her mouth to say something that she hadn't before, "You know, you are right pretty child, and you can do better. ' Don't let nobody bring you down, Kath-a –leen; especially no mane. You can do better." Ms. Clemmie worked at the City of Memphis Hospital as an assistant who cleaned surgical tools. Ms. Clemmie was so light that they called her "damn near white." The only thing that gave her away was her saying that she was black and she was proud. "Ms. Clemmie? Kathleen responded, "I'm sorry that I came home like I did, and it won't happen again. I wasn't raised that way, I really wasn't. " "I know, baby" she said, "I can tell. Most women are not raised that way, but usually somebody, some mane, comes along and makes us forget our raising. I know. It happened to me; to both of my daughters and most of the women in the world. I got to get my bus."

Ms. Clemmie's advice was sticking, but Kathleen was determined to shake it off. What did she know about Ernest? What made her think that he was not good enough for her? Ms. Clemmie did not understand that Ernest was not like other men. Then Kathleen's attention got fixed to her physical state. Why was she hurting so badly? She wanted to talk to Shug without telling her what she had done, but there was no way. Kathleen would have to confess that she gave up her virginity. Maybe she could tell her why she could hardly close her legs and why she was still having an issue of blood. She walked over to Dorothy's bed and shook her. "Hey, Shug wake up, I want to ask you something." Dorothy turned over and put one finger up as she ran to the restroom to get the remnants of the tobacco from her mouth. She actually slept with a little piece in her mouth. When Dorothy returned Kathleen told her what happened and how it hurt. "Supposed to hurt, girl, that's why it's called 'breaking in. 'I ain't never heard nobody say 'easing in.' Kathleen related how she was still bleeding some and continuing to hurt. " How big is he, girl? Seeing that Kathleen could not answer, she picked up a new pencil from the nightstand and asked if he was as long as that, which was about 7 inches. "No, he was longer than that. I only saw it when he went to the bathroom and it looked like a big old fat black cucumber," Kathleen explained. "Have mercy, have mercy, girl, it's the wonder you can even talk, let alone walk. Did he use some Vaseline?" Kathleen shook her head "no". "Did he use his finger to get you wet before he put it in? Kathleen again shook her head from side to side. "Did you use your finger to... forget it, I know you didn't. You ain't supposed to let no man do nothing to you for the first time until you are wet enough or make him use some Vaseline or jelly to ease the pain. It's the wonder you didn't have to have stitches big as you said he was. Girl, you really don't know shit, do you? Kathleen was ashamed, but felt the need to tell her more "Shug, I didn't even know that you were supposed to open your legs. I thought that a man was supposed to get on top of you and...and it would be like ...like friction, you know, rubbing the naked parts together. I know he must have thought that I was stupid. He may not ever call me again. He's probably used to more experienced girls." Dorothy reassured her that most men who break in a girl will always come back. "They like to know that they are the first, girl, don't you know that? But it really ain't no picnic for them either." Shug laughed a bit before confessing, "I had two guys who thought that they were the first, and kept coming back." They both laughed, as Kathleen reacted with, "Aw, Shug, girl." Kathleen settled took a long hot bath and then went to bed. Deep down she wondered if it was her last time to see Ernest. Was it as painful for him as it was for her? Did he really like it or was he moaning because she was so bad in bed? Would he call her, or was it all over because she wasn't a "good girl" anymore?

Kathleen could not stop asking herself questions. She was becoming consumed by thoughts of Ernest; any thought of completing her education was gradually fading without her realizing it. One reason her mother discouraged exclusive or steady dating was that it could lead to sex or early marriage. Contrary to this, when Lucinda became ill, a husband was exactly what she wanted for Kathleen in the form of Jimmy Lee, so that her daughter would be cared for after she died. Lucinda's fear was what had just happened to Kathleen, but the odds against her relationship with Ernest leading to a marriage proposal would probably be slim to none.

Getting back to Rockville Center brought some semblance of comfort to Kathleen. Even though she had been living there for a short period, it seemed a place of sanctuary. Part of her would probably always feel alone, but she wouldn't be lonely. Mrs. Fasse, however imposing, had taken a liking to her and likewise. They talked about her visit with Dorothy, being careful to leave off the part about Dr. Shaeffer's attempt to take girlie pictures of her. Instead, Kathleen focused on the satisfaction she felt from Mrs. Fasse's choice of her over Dorothy as their housekeeper, and how she apparently cared about her welfare. While talking with her about the size of the mansion, the pool and the bus ride, Kathleen knew that it would not be long before she told Mrs. Fasse the whole truth and nothing but. Deception was not a welcome characteristic to Kathleen, and she was not going to continue it, because she really liked Mrs. Fasse and the rest of the family. "Why don't you sleep for an hour longer, Minnie? Mr. Fasse is not going into the office until late afternoon, and Teddy doesn't start back to school until next week. We're really glad that you're with us,

Ruby O'Gray

dear." As Mrs. Fasse was leaving her room, Minnie had to say something to her. "Ms. Fasse, would you…would you call me Katy, please, it's what my mother used to call me? I'll explain why later. " Ms. Fasse walked toward her, held her cheeks and kissed her on the forehead, "Yes, I'll be happy to, Katy."

A month had passed and Kathleen was getting the hang of life in the suburbs. On her days off, she would take long walks on one side of the street and walk back on the other. One day she went as far as Oceanside, and saw a beach nearby. She put on her shades and the one pair of patent leather high heels she owned. Heels made Kathleen look taller and she drew lots of attention from passersby; men slowed down while driving and smiling or whistling. Kathleen just wanted to look grown up. One day she walked as far as Woolworth's, which was about twelve blocks away. She was being stared at from the time she entered until she got to the counter. Looking around her, Kathleen noticed that she was the only dark spot in the sea of rice, and possibly seemed out of place to the people in that part of town. She did not have a maid's uniform on, but had on a red fitted skirt and a white knit shell. She had rinsed her hair to a light auburn and it hung orderly on her shoulders. People stared and some were whispering as she passed them. Kathleen wondered if her underwear was showing or she had a hole somewhere. She wanted to exit as quickly as possible, but she knew that she needed the toilet items that she was buying. Suddenly, a woman touched her on the shoulder and asked her a question that she would not have expected to hear in a million years, "Excuse me, but could I have your autograph? We understand that you're incognito, but it's hard not to recognize one of the Supremes." Kathleen, laughed and told

88

her that she was not one of the Supremes, but thanked her for thinking so. The woman whispered, "If you say so, but would you mind singing a little of that *Stop in the Name of Love*, just so I could be sure?" Oddly enough, Kathleen accommodated the lady by singing a few lines of the song. She knew that she could sing, but she also knew that she didn't sound like the Supremes. The lady announced to all the people that she was not a Supreme, and she then told Kathleen that she knew how to keep a secret. She, too, had been in show business and understood why she could not reveal who she was- she had been a Flora Dora Girl, whatever that was. When Kathleen left, the lady followed her in her car to the apartment building. She waved goodbye and Kathleen waved back. She smiled at the wackiness of the situation and told Mrs. Fasse as soon as she walked in. Teddy asked her to sing after he heard what happened at the grocer's. Kathleen sang Dionne Warwick's *Message to Micheal* to the delight of Teddy and Mrs. Fasse. Teddy was in a kind of daze while she sang. He laid back on the bed as Kathleen's soothing voice put a smile on both members of her captive audience. Her voice had a richness and sincerity; she always had it; even as early as five years old when she imitated actors from the old Busby Berkeley musicals. "You could be on Broadway in a musical if you wanted. Mom, we need to get her an agent so she can be famous. Whad 'ya say, Minnie?" After Teddy's outburst of enthusiasm, Minnie rubbed his head and said thanks, but she told him maybe she would try when she got some vocal training. They continued to rave over her singing until it was time for them to retire for the evening.

Around midnight, there was a faint knock at her door; she got up and opened the door only to see Teddy standing there with his finger over his lips "shush" position. Kathleen was reluctant to let him in, but did so anyway. She did not close the door completely, as she knew this was not an easily explainable situation if caught by her employers. Teddy found his way to the sofa and proceeded to sit down. "Minnie?" he whispered, "Would you mind if I asked you to do something for me tomorrow?" "I dunno; what something do you want?" she replied. "When Bernie comes over tomorrow, would you pretend...I mean could lie like I...kissed you and you liked it?" Kathleen remembered what she had overheard the boys saying, but did not mention it. "Why should I do that, Teddy?" Teddy seemed reluctant to answer then changed his mind. "Uh, that's alright, I was just kidding. You know, your room smells different from mine; it's even different from Mom and Dad's room. It's...it's like I just walked into a basket of flowers." Kathleen explained that it was the cologne that she wore that smelled like that. Then Teddy walked toward the door, "You can really sing, Minnie, really, and ...oh, if Bernie comes over tomorrow, forget what I said. I was just going to win some old bet with him. He bet me that you wouldn't kiss a blind guy, and I told him that you were not prejudiced against blind guys; that's all. I should never have asked you to do that. G'night, Minnie, sleep tight, we don't have bedbugs, but watch out for other things that might bite."

Teddy made a quick exit, and Kathleen laughed, wondering why he chose to come in her room and ask her that question. She turned off the television, clicked on the small night light on the table, walked over to the sofa and decided to call Memphis; when she picked up the phone she heard Teddy's voice. "No, she didn't kiss me, but it's not because I was blind, it was because...because she has never kissed a white boy... Sure I told her that I was Jewish, but she didn't understand that...Look, you can't say things like that about her. Minnie's not...she's not like that...No, she won't take money from you or anybody. 'Just kiss my ass, asshole!" Teddy slammed the phone down after his sharp defense of Minnie and to her delight. She wondered if he was respecting her because she spent time talking and listening to him each day. Teddy had become a teacher to her, of sorts, showing her how to use the ham radio, explaining the many gadgets he had from devices that could turn off his lights- and how to run the stereo. Kathleen wondered, was it because she made his sandwiches with the trimmed crusts. She noticed that Teddy's demeanor changed ever since she sang. Teddy was almost in a trance when he heard Kathleen's voice. Whatever it was that made him stop talking about her in a sexual manner and made him defend her, Kathleen was thankful. That night, she went to bed smiling and planned to sing more often, while doing housework. From that day on, there was nothing that either wouldn't do for the other. Kathleen felt that bonding with Teddy was like having a new brother with the old ideals and unwritten rules that went along with being siblings. Little did Teddy know how truly close in age they were; perhaps, Kathleen thought, that was why they bonded. Even so, she recollected her mother saying, "A boy the same age as a girl will never be as mature as the girl." Teddy would soon be fifteen, Kathleen was just eighteen. Kathleen turned off all the lights in her room and counted backwards from 500 until she went to sleep. This was the first night that Ernest was not the first thing or major player on her mind. This was the first night that Kathleen would not cry herself to sleep.

CHAPTER III

One Error and No One Left On Base

It was Saturday morning and Mrs. Fasse was intent on speaking with Kathleen. "You really think that you have put one over on me, don't you, young lady, but I have been around a long time and I can spot fear anywhere!" Kathleen began breathing very hard, frightened she'd been found out. Before she could say anything, Ms. Fasse sternly continued, "You, young lady, are going to Minneola next week to get your driver's license if I have to take you dragging and screaming; there's no reason to be afraid to drive." Still nervous, Kathleen said, "Ma'am? Afraid?" Ms. Fasse continued, "Yes, afraid. Here I am leaving, and you need a driver's license for emergencies or errands that need to be run and you've made no effort to get them. We have got to get them when I come back, Minnie, you hear?" "Yes, Yes, ma'am, Mrs. Fasse, I will, Kathleen said.

Mrs. Fasse was excited to be meeting her husband in Florida for a weekend vacation. It was the first time that the two of them had been out of town together since Minnie came, and she was as nervously excited as a newborn kitten. Teddy's accident had brought with it complications from time to time that effected his respiratory system. Periodically, Teddy's breathing resembled little panic attacks that kept Mrs. Fasse on her toes; afraid to leave him. Teddy wanted his parents to have a break, an evening away of concern for him. Reluctantly, his parents admitted that they wanted likewise, so Teddy bargained with them. He would take the breathing exercises the doctor ordered if they took a vacation. Mrs. Fasse often spoke of Teddy's unfortunate accident as a blessing. She thought of his recovery as the second chance for their marriage. Mr. Fasse promised never to hurt his wife's feelings or do anything that might upset her ever if Teddy made it through the touch and go surgery. Without Mrs. Fasse fully explaining it, Kathleen gathered from her conversation that Mr. Fasse probably had had an affair at some point in their lives; probably when Teddy was first injured. Mrs. Fasse once stated, "If Teddy hadn't come around, I probably would have killed his father in Florida for the foolish...oh, well. Then of course, I would probably have died in my cell from claustrophobia or filth or some mustachioed woman named Hilda." Kathleen laughed, but also realized that Mrs. Fasse tended to use humor when speaking of unpleasant things. Going to Florida was probably a little bit of good and bad to her, because Mrs. Fasse would also get to see her sister Gladys who lived there, bit Mr. Fasse's shoe business took him down to Florida frequently- the location of his dalliance.

Kathleen and Teddy would be all alone when his parents left and the growing closeness between the two of them had not gone unnoticed by Teddy's mother. Mrs. Fasse didn't seem worried that they might have acted inappropriately, but she was about to talk about something that had not crossed the mind of either Teddy or Minnie, the housekeeper. Despite her seemingly liberal views, Mrs. Fasse was still a real-life Jewish mother- conservative in her manner, but very much concerned about her Jewish lineage. She readily accepted the union of Sammy Davis Jr. and Mai Brit, as she would say, "Sammy's a convert; really a Jew, just darker than most." Although not all orthodox, most of Mrs. Fasse's views were what she called rather conservative than reformed. Being orthodox was more the intent of her other family members. Just before she left, Mrs. Fasse needed to talk. While waiting for the Super's assistant to her luggage, she called Teddy and Minnie into the living room for a briefing of sorts. This demure woman was determined to stand while insisting that the others sit on her sofa and look her straight in the eye. "I'm looking, Ma, I'm looking," Teddy quipped. "This is not funny, young man, and that goes for you too, Minnie. I want you to take this list of numbers, and if anything should happen, I mean anything that you can't handle, call one of these. This one's the hotel where we will be staying, my sister Gladys' number, my husband's office in Florida, my sister Minnie's number, and my daughter's. You can see the names by the number. Oh. Here's Teddy's doctor's number and the pharmacist and...," Minnie had to interrupt her, or she was going to miss her flight. "Mrs. Fasse, I will take care of everything. And please, if you are worried about Teddy and me being more than friends-it ain't gonna happen. I am not like that. WE are not going to be like that." Teddy injected, "That's what you think." "Teddy!" Minnie and Mrs. Fasse yelled simultaneously. "If you keep playing like that, Teddy, someone might get the wrong impression," his mother added. "Okay, Mom, please don't miss your flight, and say hello to Dad; give him a hug, will ya? I got to go back to bed, I am tired from dreaming about sex with Minnie all night." "Teddy!" they both yelled again. This time, Mrs. Fasse hugged Minnie and left. She pointed her finger just one last time before leaving and said, "Look out for my child, please, I have never left him since-."

Kathleen went back to bed, only to have the phone ring minutes later. "What does Dorothy want this early in the morning?" she thought. Mrs. Fasse gave Kathleen her own private number after realizing that Teddy had been picking up the phone and listening to her every call. Dorothy loved to call and gossip about her employers' antics. "You still asleep girl? Wake up; have I got something to tell you," she would say. Kathleen wanted to hear, but wanted to go back to sleep more, since Mrs. Fasse had kept her and Teddy up late the night before talking. Dorothy began to tell her about her employers "open marriage" and how they both had sleeping partners over. Furthermore, Dorothy was amazed about what happened last night-Mr. and Mrs. Shaeffer slept together! Just the two of them! Dorothy could not stop laughing. "It was normal as hell up in here last night, Katy. And they' still in bed this morning. They told me to take the day off, so I thought that I might come over to your crib; how about it? Kathleen couldn't say no, even though it was not her off day. The timing was almost too perfect. With the Fasse's out of town, they had the place all to themselves. Of course, Teddy would certainly not object-this would mean another female in the house! Dorothy planned to spend the night and leave early. Kathleen knew that she needed to run this by Mrs. Fasse, so she planned to call her late that evening. It would be about two hours before Shug got there, so she climbed back into bed to get a little more shuteye. She told Teddy about the visit and asked him to wake her in about an hour.

Teddy got up and knocked on Kathleen's door after oversleeping. Jumping out of bed, she heard Teddy's alarm and the buzzer simultaneously. Teddy shut off the alarm, and Kathleen answered the door. Shug looked at both Teddy and Kathleen as only she would after seeing them in their bed clothes. Well, well, well. I hope that I am not interrupting anything. Maybe I should go back out and come later." This was typical Shug, so Kathleen began to explain the circumstances. "Come on in here girl, I went back to bed after you called, and Teddy was… wait a minute I don't have to explain anything to you, I am at home and so is Teddy. Teddy, this is my friend, I think, Dorothy, but we sometimes call her Shug…that's Sugar for short. Dorothy added, "It's a southern thing." "Dorothy, uh, Shug, this is my friend Teddy Fasse, Kathleen added. You can shake his hand, he won't bite." "Yes, I will," he quipped, "I just haven't bitten Minnie yet. So, you're going to stay the night, huh?" Dorothy told him "Yes." He tripped over her bag and fell into Kathleen's arms. "Hey what is wrong with you, Babydoll? Are you blind or something?" Tension and silence filled the room. Kathleen quickly shushed Dorothy, as Teddy beat a hasty retreat to his room and slammed the door. "Come back, Teddy, she didn't mean it; she didn't know. I never told her."

Dorothy felt about two feet tall, after realizing what she uttered from her big mouth. She knocked on Teddy's door genuinely sorry for what she had said, but having a keen understanding of the male animal, she decided to approach him in a totally unexpected way. "Look, Teddy, if I knew that you were blind, I would never have said that so don't blame Ka…Minnie for what I said. Anyway, you may not be able to see me, but I certainly would like to see you again. You are one good-looking white boy. Now, down home if I said that, they would be ready to put me in jail for soliciting, but then I know that you are used to hearing that. No wonder Minnie won't come over to my house on her day off; she' 'round here looking at you." Kathleen started to interrupt her and Dorothy put her hand over her mouth. Look, I came over to visit Minnie, but if you want to stay in there all day and miss out on dancing with me, then, well, that's your choice. But if I were a teen-aged boy, I would be ready and willing for the opportunity to hold on to a real woman for a change, and believe me, I am a REAL woman. I know you don't get a chance to do that too often, do you?" There was silence for a moment then Dorothy repeated, "Do you?" Taking advantage of the silence, Dorothy finally spoke, "Well, Minnie, I guess I may as well call and find out when the next bus is coming, I don't want to stay where I am not wanted. Where is your phone?" As Dorothy walked to Kathleen's room, she continued to express her sorrow for speaking out of turn, but she also continued mentioning Teddy's good looks. A slow creaking of a door prompted the girls to look around and there stood Teddy in the doorway opening his mouth, "Do you really think that I am good-looking?" "Honey, if you looked any better I would have to call in the pretty police, because it's a crime for a man to look as good as you do. How old are you anyway, 16, 17?" Dorothy knew exactly what to do to get his attention and continued to do so. Kathleen marveled at Shug's expertise. Ever since the two of them met, she envied Shug's ability to read men, even though Shug always seemed to lower her standards when it came to what men wanted. Shug was free and uninhibited sexually; bordering on being called immoral, since nothing deterred her from dating a man who was taken; even a married one. Kathleen wondered from time to time if Shug had been involved with the Shaeffers, but was reluctant to ask. Anyway, no matter what the answer, Shug would justify her actions and never change. Kathleen also noticed how Teddy was impressed with the compliments Dorothy was showering on him.

Kathleen fixed pancakes and scrambled eggs for Dorothy, while Teddy impressed Dorothy by pouring syrup and cutting the pancakes. He could feed himself without trouble and wanted Dorothy to know that. Kathleen thought, if he could only see her, he might not feel the same, since Dorothy was no raving beauty. Yet, Teddy, like most other men, was being swayed by Dorothy's charm. Teddy was blind and her charm was judged by ears only and not eyes.

After breakfast, Kathleen resumed her daily chores and planned an outing with Teddy. The nickname Shug was fun for him to say, and Teddy did often while fished for more compliments from her. Whether they were true wasn't important. Like all other teens, he liked the attention. The two of them went to his room to dance. This didn't sit too well with Kathleen, for pangs of jealousy were hitting her left and right. Kathleeen asked herself, "How dare she come over and try to take over her people?" She watched as Dorothy allowed him to put his arms around her while she actually had him moving to the beat; literally following her feet. Of course it was a good thing that Teddy was experiencing- dancing, socializing, having fun- but why did it have to be with Shug? About ten minutes after Kathleen stopped watching them and resumed her chores, Shug called for her to come to the room. She answered with reluctance, "I'm real busy trying to finish cleaning this bathroom; what do you want?" Shug begged her to come to Teddy's room, and she finally did. When she walked to the door, there stood Teddy with his hand outstretched. "May I have this dance, Madame Minnie?" Shug was gesturing for her to accept, while holding the record she was about to play on the stereo. Shug put a record on by Frank Sinatra from Teddy's mother's collection of songs. They began dancing, and Kathleen followed Teddy's lead, surprised at how he moved. His blindness became a moot factor as Teddy moved with ease, gliding around the floor, eventually trying to dip Kathleen, they both fell on the floor. They laughed and hugged each other, as Shug fell on the floor too. "Ya'll ain't gonna be playing on the floor without me." That incident sealed Shug's fate as Teddy's new friend, and reassured Kathleen's position as Teddy's truest friend. Teddy went through the dance lesson to please Kathleen, and she knew it. The rest of the evening they talked about sex, food, the Beatles, Motown, and debated about the stolen talents of Black singers by Whites. Teddy's friends periodically phoned and asked if they could come over, but Teddy coughed, fabricated something, or pretended to be sick or contagious so they would stay away. He was not about to share his kingdom this day, because his subjects were real women who spoiled him with every complimentary word or rubbed his brow. Teddy was feeling his manhood, in more ways than one, and as Shug noted, "You won't let your friend come over, because you don't want someone throwing a hitch in your git-a-long. Smart man, Teddy. Smart man."

Teddy and the girls talked late into the night about life, love, and the pursuit of happiness, while eating popcorn, kosher hotdogs, french fries, and soda pop. Around seven o'clock, his parents called and asked how things were. "Mom, when you get back, we are going to have to listen to your favorite record by Sinatra. I used to think that guy was square, but thanks to Minnie, I have a new perception of him…Yes, everything is going great here, and you and Dad?…Good, now, Mom, we have to go, we've got things to do…Just things, Mom. We're looking at TV and listening to music and… we're in her room and Dorothy is here. Dorothy, Minnie's friend who came to New York with her…Why? They gave her the day off and …no, mom, please? Okay, alright, already, I'm going to my room. She's going to call me on my phone. Mom is bugging the shit out of me about Dorothy." Teddy went to his room as fast as he could and picked up the phone. Kathleen hesitantly put the other one down, regretting that she instead of Teddy had not told Mrs. Fasse about Dorothy spending the night. She was the adult in the situation, and Mrs. Fasse trusted her to act accordingly. She feared that she had given the Fasse's a reason to fire her, so she was preparing for the worst, but hoping for the best. She told herself to expect either a pink slip or a chastising when the Fasse's returned. Seeing Kathleen upset, Shug asked, "You didn't tell her that I was spending the night?" Kathleen answered, "No, I was really going to, but I just hadn't gotten around to it." Suddenly Teddy was yelling like a madman, "WHAT,

WHAT THE HELL DOES THAT MEAN, MOM? You think we're screwing around, don't you? Well, contrary to what you think, Minnie doesn't do that. I know you didn't say that she did, but that's what you were thinking. Look, Ma…I'm sorry; please, don't cry… please. I didn't mean to… Dad, you know How Mom imagines things. We're really having a nice time…yes…yes, sir…no, I wouldn't lie to you; you know that. Okay…Mom, I'm sorry, I didn't mean to yell at you. I shouldn't have lost my temper; I apologize. I love you too. Just don't think the worst all the time; the worst of Minnie, too. She's my friend, and she's not like what you' thinking…I'll see you in two days- yeah, kiss, kiss." Kathleen was standing in the doorway when Teddy was about to leave the room, but he seemed to know that she was near and he asked, "You heard right?" "Yeah, I couldn't help but hear as loud as you were. I should have called her and told her like I started to," Minnie lamented. Teddy said, "Fuck it! Let's just forget about Mom and Dad tonight. They'll have time to cool off, so when they get back things will be groovy. Now, where were we? Oh, yeah, there's a scary movie on tonight that I want to watch. Dorothy could not hold her peace any longer about a subject that she was reluctant to ask, "Look here, Teddy Baby, I want to know one thing. Why do you listen to the television, I mean, you can't see it, so why put yourself through that?" Immediately, Kathleen leaped to his defense, angered and wondering why Shug would ask Teddy such a question, but Teddy was cool and more assertive and gave an unusual reply. "I can't see you, but I can hear and imagine what you look like or what you're doing. I don't always know, but I can feel and the rest, well, somebody can tell me. Blind people are just like everybody else, just missing one thing. I haven't always been blind, you know. Sit down, and I'll tell you how it happened," he said. "Wait a minute, how did you know that I was standing?" Shug asked. "Imagination, and anyway, most of the time, I can tell by the way your voice carries. If I'm standing and you sound like you're under me, then you're sitting, if I'm sitting and your voice sounds above me, then you're standing. It's simple, you know, nothing magic. Everybody likes to think that blind people have some sixth sense or magical power that makes them know more than anybody. I don't know about other people, but I guess I listen more because I can't see. Are you sitting now?" Simultaneously they said, "Yes" and listened carefully as he told them the story of how he became blind.

Teddy talked for about twenty minutes or so, first asking if the girls liked sports and ending with the loss of his eyesight. When he finished Kathleen cried. Both Kathleen and Shug felt compelled to tell stories about the blind people they knew; funny stories about other blind talented people who lived in the neighborhoods to lighten the mood, but Teddy handled that. He asked them to go to the living room where the small white player piano stood and he sat down to play. The girls were amazed how he played *Rhapsody in Blue* from memory. They applauded and kissed him on both cheeks. Shug complimented him with, "Boy, you are just like Stevie Wonder or Ray Charles." Teddy turned so red with embarrassment and smiled the biggest smile. Shug couldn't help but comment; she was so impressed, "You have so much talent; if I could play like that, I would be on the Ed Sullivan Show or playing at that Car-knee-gee Hall place. I don't always like that highbrow stuff, but the way you play makes you feel something, don't it, Katy? There was what seemed like a long silence before Teddy responded with, "Katy? "I mean Minnie? You know, uh, we always call her Katy back home; it… it was a nickname one of her relatives gave her…. right, Katy? Look, it's late and I have to get back to work tomorrow by ten o'clock, so, show me where to let it lay, girl, Shug quickly added. She knew that she had opened up a can of worms that Kathleen would have to close. Would Teddy suspect that Minnie was not her real name, distrust her, tell his mother? Kathleen knew that Teddy was a bright kid, but maybe he would think nothing of what Shug said. Kathleen stared at Shug and shook her head in regret and said, "Let my sofa bed out and sleep on the far side, and I'm sleeping near the door. And don't chew any strange food before going to sleep. The bath is right here, the towels are in that linen closet. Teddy, I'm going to turn in too. Can I get anything for you?" He replied, "No Katy. Katy… yeah, I like that better. Do you mind? Minnie sounds like my aunt." Kathleen told him yes, but thought it best that he not say it around his parents until she explained why. He agreed, said goodnight, and went to bed.

After the girls settled in, Shug began to talk about how she missed home and planned to go back after she had saved up some money. Then Teddy's accident became the topic of conversation. "Imagine that. The boy could see until a few years ago. I don't know how many times I have seen people get hit with bats while playing ball and nothing happened except they were left with a big goose egg or a scar. Getting hit between the eyes with a bat, going into a coma and waking up blind is about as cold a hand that life can deal you; that poor baby." Kathleen added, "He's not a baby, and he's definitely not poor, but he is bright and smart as a whip.

103

It won't be long now before he finds out about who I really am, that I'm Kathleen, and that social security number his mother has does not fit my name. When the time comes for her to send the quarters in, she'll know. I don't know if I can stay here and watch him be disappointed in me like that. I really like the boy. I mean, he's like a brother, almost. I am going to have to tell him one day…soon, I know." They turned out the light, and almost as soon as her head hit the pillow, Shug went to sleep. It was hard for Kathleen to go, for she was bracing herself for a change.

The next morning Shug left around eight o'clock to catch the early bus. She hugged Teddy before leaving and promised to call later. Teddy went back to bed, but Kathleen wanted to go to Waulbaum's and pick up some fresh swordfish. She had grown fond of the way Ms. Fasse taught her to cook, and Teddy liked it too. She asked him to call his friend Bernie later on, so that she could go shopping, or get up and go with her- something she knew that he would not do. Just as she was about to clean her room, the phone rang. It was Ms. Fasse asking how things were and if her little friend was still there. Kathleen answered her questions and apologized for not telling her that Dorothy had come over for the night. She told her that she intended to do it, and that it would never happen again. Mrs. Fasse had little to say about it, asked her if she needed any more money for marketing – to which she replied "No," and the conversation ended. Teddy emerged from his door, dressed and ready to walk to the market- something he hadn't done in years. Kathleen was pleasantly surprised, and the prospect of getting him out of the house added to her joy. Waulbaum's was just at the corner, and for Teddy to trust Kathleen to walk at all meant a lot. She quickly got ready, locked the door to the apartment, and entered the elevator, smiling. "I'm glad that you trust me enough to go with me, Ted, I am very, very honored." Teddy added in a British accent, "Think nothing of it, M'lady, the king sometimes travels with his subjects, so people will know that kings are groovy too." They laughed and walked outside, down the street, and Kathleen made certain that she was walking on the curbside. She was so careful, not wanting him to be afraid. Teddy dominated the conversation with immaterial questions, or what Kathleen's grandmother would call, "talking just to be talking." Out of nowhere, Teddy asked her what is the best and the worst thing about kissing. She replied, "The best is when a man knows how, and it curls your toes; the worst is when they try to stick their tongue down your throat until you choke." She wondered why he asked that, but was not ready to further this line of conversation by asking why. Minnie did not want her employer's son leading into things that might prove inappropriate or uncomfortable.

It was so early, and this was not a neighborhood where people got up on weekends early. Kathleen knew that this was why Teddy consented to go, but whatever the reason Teddy reverted to his childhood and squeezed himself inside the basket while she bought the fish. No store manager or employee said anything to them, because they all recognized Mrs. Fasse's boy and smiled. Afterwards, they walked back taking their time. Teddy seemed more comfortable coming back, as Minnie tactfully told him when they were about to step off a curb or if someone was in front of them. "Curb at twelve o'clock in four steps, flower pot at one o'clock in two steps, doors with middle grip at chest range-ahead in about six steps, pull and walk-hold on to my waist and turn right to the elevator after ten steps." The slow moving elevator always gave Kathleen time to think. She thought how she and Ted starting making a game of everything. Standing close to him, Kathleen could feel Teddy's heart racing. They were both quiet as tears welled up in her eyes, but she did not let one drop, for Kathleen was ecstatic that someone really cared about and needed her; this was not Minnie, but Kathleen. This was Kathleen who cared for her mother, Kathleen, who cared for her sisters and brothers, Kathleen who knew that they all loved her; this was Kathleen, who also cared for Ernest, but probably never really cared for her.

"Don't you get tired of going to the same place every time we go out, honey? I mean, we always go to a drive-in or a movie and then to bed. Why don't we go some-place else, or a dance, to a club or house party? You don't let me be around your friends, because you say you don't have any, but you have to see those same friends every Saturday night." Kathleen's tone, when she questioned Ernest, had begun to sound like a bored child who wanted a change of scenery from the TV to a movie. It was five weeks since Kathleen lost her virginity, and it appeared that since the conquest, Ernest just enjoyed taking her to bed and hanging with his drinking buddies, who frequently talked about chasing women right in front of her. Kathleen didn't have enough experience with men to know that men treat you the way they want until you let them know early on how to treat you. At times, they were like little boys in adult clothing.

Kathleen had made the mistake of letting Ernest think that she could not exist without him; that he was the center of her world. She had forgotten about school or learning how to do anything, and even stopped reading. Kathleen always loved to sew, and used the machine that Dorothy's grandmother had to create any dress that was in a fashion magazine, obviously for a lot less money. Kathleen frequented fabric stores, but when women in the neighborhood heard about her sewing ability, they hired her to make choir or party dresses. She even hand sewed with the final product looking as if it came out of a shop. Making doll clothes since she was eight, Kathleen continued sewing with one semester of Home Economics in Junior High School, but no matter how secure her talented Kathleen was with needle and thread, she wasn't secure in how to fix her relationship with Ernest.

This evening, Kathleen heard a surprising set of words flowing out of Ernest's mouth; words that sounded similar to the ones Ms. Clemmie warned that she might hear one day. "Look, uh, baby, maybe we should not see each other for a while. I mean, I think maybe that we need some space and time to miss each other, okay? Maybe see other people to see how we feel about each other. I'm starting to feel like I'm in a closet, baby, with no way out. I...uh, I can't function like that. Like you told me you just wanted to run from things, you understand?" Even then Kathleen could not tell him what she thought, she was afraid, so she said, "Maybe you're right." He had begun to do things that she ignored-things like tell her he was going to pick her up at seven and not show up until ten or eleven. Even if she was in bed, she would still get up after listening to his sorry ass excuse for not being on time. Each time this happened, Kathleen choice was against what she really felt. She felt that Ernest was taking her for granted, lost respect for her, but most of all, she had lost respect for herself. Her loneliness took precedence over her true feelings. She just didn't want to be alone. Kathleen thought that if she should have a husband, it should be Ernest, because he had seen her naked, and she had told him her inner most feelings about her mother and family, and surely he and no other man would understand her like that- ever. He was her first, and she was bound and determined for him to be the last man who saw her naked. Seeing someone naked was a big thing in Kathleen's family; even her grandmother bragged about the fact that she never got completely naked for her own husband. She would say, "If a man sees everything you got, there's no mystery, and if he gets what he wants every time he wants it, you might as well forget about him wanting it after a while." She had heard her talk with her sister about "the grip" and how that could send a man up a wall. She wondered if she had "the grip" and maybe that's why Ernest did not want her anymore.

That night, Kathleen went home without making love, and sat on the porch thinking about how Ernest really did not want or need her. He wanted a few weeks of just being alone, to see other people to test if he and Kathleen really had something going on. Kathleen reluctantly agreed, but Kathleen made up her mind to make love to him one more time, and use "the grip". She would read anything about sex that she could get a hold of, resist Ernest's late night invitations, and go to parties or out with other guys who were always asking her. Maybe then, Ernest would understand how much he wanted and needed her. She was willing to gamble anything to make him jealous. Kathleen always tried to resist her sensual side, because she was afraid of being labeled a "fast" girl or a loose woman, but this was a desperate situation and it called for desperate measures. She knew that the **Sexolog**y book that she had read confirmed "the grip;" it involved the vagina tightening around the penis, like a woman would if she was trying to hold then quickly to release her urine but not release it. A few of those, like the book said, would surely make Ernest Kathleen's "love slave," or so she thought. She planned to climb up on top of him- his favorite position, and give him the ride of his life. It would also involve her talking dirty to him and telling him what to do. She practiced, as if writing a script. He seemed to respond to this once when Kathleen told him in the heat of passion to "grab my ass; call me baby." He was like putty saying, "Okay, baby, okay bitch, yeah, yeah." She didn't care what he called her in bed, as long as he called. If she hadn't covered his mouth, someone would have called the police for disturbing the peace. That night, he told her how much he loved her, and that she was the best he had ever had. A sense of power came over Kathleen, but she felt ashamed for acting like the "fast" girls that she had always heard her grandma talk about. She thought, maybe next time she'd make him act like her slave-like she'd read about. Of course, Kathleen thought, he would surely ask her to be his wife after all that. She had it all worked out in her head, her heart, but she didn't really think about what Ernest had in his mind. Just in case that didn't work, Kathleen was prepared to unleash the green-eyed monster-jealousy. After much thought, Kathleen decided that jealousy would surely nail Ernest, and she wouldn't have to screw him first to make it happen.

Two doors down from the house on Greenwood lived a Mrs. Weston, whose son was just back from Vietnam. He had seen Dorothy before he left and Kathleen since he had returned, but had asked Dorothy out, figuring he could make love with her before being shipped off. Dorothy promised to go out with him, but gave up nothing. She did promise to write him and go out with him when he got back. The letters he received were so flowery, clear and inviting. The words used would make any man anticipate a night with the woman who wrote it, even if he had never seen her. Francis was his name, a girl's name to most, but upon his return, when he knocked on the door where Dorothy lived, the kids laughed when he announced his name. "Francis is here Shug" they would say in a nursery rhyme tone. The cadence continued until she came to the door. Francis was armed with the letters, and he asked to take her out that night. She would not leave the safety of the screened door, because he looked as if he was going to devour her. Here was a man who had returned from Vietnam with expectations of sex with Shug, which would have been all right, as this was the intent according to the teasing letters. Shug told him that she would be ready at seven; so pick her up then. She went back and explained the date to Kathleen, but urged Kathleen not to sit around on a Friday night waiting for Ernest to call her. Kathleen told her that she was going the next street over to James' place, who was throwing a party for his girlfriend, and she would get a chance to play cards, which she loved to do. Ironically, James lived on James Street, and Kathleen knew that she could have a good time there. There would be dancing between games and lots of laughter; enough to divert her thoughts of Ernest. Kathleen wished Shug well and finished the hem on the tight blue dress that she was making. Shug tried to get her to go on a double date, as Francis mentioned that he had a friend, but she declined the invitation. She asked that no one tell Ernest where she was if he called. She figured that two or three time being unavailable and using "the grip" like she did the last time they were together, might get him back on the right track with a definite proposal.

Seven o'clock came. Kathleen ran into Francis on the way out who gave a wolf whistle and a smile, as she switched down the stairs, across the street and through the shortcut to James' house. Kathleen learned from Dorothy to hold her stomach in and her butt and chest out enough to rejuvenate a 90 year old man. In that tight blue dress, there was no imagination about her womanly blessings. James was like a brother to Katy, and she was careful to treat his girlfriend like a sister to avoid jealousy. They were not women who cheated with each other's men, and some were confident, like James' girlfriend. She was not above introducing Shug or Kathleen to available men from time to time, and Kathleen and Dorothy understood that it was to protect her relationship with James. Well into dealing the ninth game of Tonk, and after a couple of hours of dance and laughter, Kathleen wanted to find out if Ernest had called, but she didn't dare. She fought every urge within her to call Dorothy's house or him. Kathleen had a mission to accomplish.

James and his girlfriend went to their bedroom, leaving Kathleen with the other guests. The couple was getting married, and they used every opportunity to "play house" whenever they could, with no shame at all. A guy asked Kathleen to dance to "What Becomes of the Broken Hearted," but well into the dance, someone tapped the guy on the shoulder. Kathleen looked up and it was Francis. "Hey what? You and Dorothy decided to come to the dance?" She asked. Francis replied, "No 'just me. I came to dance with you; with the girl who wrote those letters." Kathleen pulled back from him and started to walk away very fast, when the guy she just danced with asked what was wrong. Kathleen assured him that everything was all right, but she had to go and tell the hosts she would call them later. Francis followed her, and asked her not to run away. "Please, don't I...I... didn't mean to upset you. I have my car, would you mind if we rode around and just talked? Dorothy is at the Paradise. I left her there. She said that she wanted to go dancing, and our date was over. There's really nothing between us, nothing at all. I should have known that it was you the minute I heard you speak. No disrespect to your friend, but she sounds like she has about as much sense as it takes to pour piss out of a boot or less." Kathleen was fiercely loyal to her friend, and quickly put him in his place. "Don't talk about Dorothy like that! She's like my sister, and you don't really know her. Just because she didn't want to be with you does not make her dumb. You men always think that you know a woman, but you don't know shit!" Kathleen was walking off when he reached out for her arm and apologized. "I didn't mean to insult her or you. I just meant that the way she talked, spoke, well, I could tell that she couldn't have put the words together that I read. Anyway, she told me that she's interested in someone else. I really like her as a person, a friend, but not-." Francis pulled out one letter that looked worn as if it had been read a number of times. "Please, can we go and sit in my car? She went reluctantly. Now, if you would just do one thing for me, I would appreciate it. Would you close your eyes and listen to this, please." Kathleen reluctantly folded her arms and listened while Francis began to read:

Page 2…Today was a touchy day for me. I read such awful things in the paper about Vietnam and the men who were fighting there. One of my classmates was killed recently, and I thought about you. I thought about you all day and how much you must miss home, a warm bed, a good meal, and a hot female body close to you. I said to myself that the day you come home, I want to give you one of those things. Then I'll get you a flower. Women don't always do that- give men flowers, I mean. I think that any man who has fought some dumb war that none of us understands and faced death, danger, and ugliness like I could never imagine, should get a flower to remember the beauty in life. Chances are you and I will see each other. I've willed it so. So, I'll be waiting for you with at least one of the three things I mentioned.

"Now, how could any man not want to be with a woman who writes like that? And you're cut as can be, you know?" Kathleen smiled and tried to deter his advances with a simple question, "What if the woman had looked like, like a real dog? I bet that woulda made you think twice about asking for a date, right?" Francis quickly answered, "When you go to a place where people lose their eyes, their legs, arms and worse, what you look like becomes less important than how that person makes you feel. I could have come back with no eyes or one arm." Kathleen looked at him, and agreed to sit in the car for a moment. Another car, pulled up across the street from them almost immediately, and turned out the lights, but neither noticed. Francis wanted Kathleen, but he knew that she was not an "easy" girl, so they sat and talked about Vietnam, his three-week furlough and her. Kathleen was fascinated; not realizing that almost an hour had passed. She told Francis that maybe she would go out with him sometime, but don't think she was giving up anything.

113

Kathleen then apologized for the letters and leading him on, but she just wanted to help her friend, make a soldier happy who was doing such a dangerous job, and to make someone feel wanted.

Francis got out and opened the door for Kathleen when she said that she was tired and wanted to turn in. As he walked her toward the house, across the street, a tall male figure stood smoking a cigarette, while leaning against the car. He coughed a bit and continued staring as Francis helped Kathleen up the stairs to the front door. He kissed her on the hand then her cheek, expressing his desire to take her out on the next night to which she replied, "Call me tomorrow, and we'll see." He looked back at her, waved, got into his car and zoomed down the street for parts unknown instead of going back home. Kathleen waved back; the figure walked to the end of the driveway and put out the cigarette with his foot. He folded his arms and stared at the door that she had just closed, then made an about face, got into his car and drove away. On the other side of the door Kathleen's smile was as the cat that swallowed the canary. She knew that the figure standing in her driveway was Ernest, and that he had seen her with Francis. All she would have to do now is wait- wait for the call that was sure come. Kathleen felt that the call may not come the next day, but very soon. Francis was a very rugged, attractive guy, and Ernest could clearly see that. The charming kiss on the hand and cheek that Francis gave her was just enough to upset Ernest and satisfy Kathleen's plan, or so she thought.

The next morning before seven-thirty, the phone rang with an invitation to breakfast, that Kathleen readily accepted. Saturday mornings in Dorothy's grand-mother's house usually consisted of hot biscuits, scrambled eggs, grits and coffee-with no meat. Kathleen usually helped with the cooking, but this morning she asked Ms. Clemmie if she could have a rain check on helping, because she had a breakfast date. "It's good to see you get up from here and go, child, 'cause a young woman don't really have no business out all night meeting the sunshine with a fella at the breakfast table unless she married to him or about to be. I hope you and that Ernest have a good breakfast, honey, 'cause that's 'bout all that scoundbugger is gonna give you." Kathleen smiled, kissed her on the cheek and informed her that Ernest would not be her breakfast date-Frank would. Ms. Clemmie had such a smile on her face after hearing this news, she told her, "You go on now, and have a good time-have one for me, too."

Kathleen answered the doorbell dressed in shorts and a sleeveless top, sandals and a purse, her hair in a ponytail and little make-up. She wanted to discourage Francis' advances by looking as plain as possible, but it seemed to no avail. Frank asked in a charming manner, "How can a woman wake up and look like this in the morning? I had gotten used to seeing the ugly mugs of hard legs in the barracks and trenches, that I almost forgot how good a woman can look." Kathleen thanked him and glanced at all the windows in the house that were stuffed with the faces of Dorothy's sisters and cousins, who grinned and smiled as she left the porch for Francis' car. He opened the door for her, and as she was putting her last leg in, Francis let out a wolf whistle. He immediately apologized to her when Kathleen froze and stared at him, and headed towards the Gridiron restaurant that was downtown.

115

Francis explained on the way of his intention to spend time with Kathleen until he went back overseas, and Kathleen told him that she would consider dating him, but that she did have a boyfriend. She told him about how they were not really getting along well at the moment. He asked her to call him Frank, and soon brought up his story of a party with his Army buddies to celebrate making it out of Vietnam. Some had wives and others girlfriends who had awaited their coming, and they would be there. He wondered if she would consider going with him to the function; it was a semi-formal affair, and he was willing to spring for her dress. Frank was light-complexioned, about five feet nine, nice looking, articulate, but he was not Ernest. She asked him why he wanted her to go with him, and not Shug or some other woman. He just said that he wanted to be with her; no one else. Kathleen was not aware of it, but Frank had done what a lot of soldier's had done at war- read the letters to his buddies, and bragged about the woman who wrote them. It was time to show her off and save face; to look good before the guys. Frank explained, "I don't expect you to act like we slept together, just come to the dance with me, please. I would appreciate it very much, and if you want me to explain it to your boyfriend, I will-" She interrupted. "No, I don't have to ask his permission, we're not married, and I'm sure he's doing whatever he wants; probably things I wouldn't approve of or will never know about. Yes, I'll go. You may have to get the dress, since I'm sure that I don't have anything nice enough." Frank was grateful and elated, but little did he know that he was doing Kathleen a favor that would ultimately change the course of her relationship with Ernest. Frankly, Frank didn't care; he was just glad to be taking Kathleen.

Frank and Kathleen walked all around town to varied stores- Three Sisters, Lerner's and others, but both agreed that none fit the occasion. Frank wanted her to have on something that would put the other ladies to shame. Kathleen had wondered why Frank wore his military clothing, but was about to learn the advantage of doing so.

Goldsmith's was one of the finest stores in Memphis, and Kathleen was excited to go there, having only been there a few times in her life just to look around. A little old white saleswoman approached them and was very accommodating and guided them to the ladies department. They explained the occasion to her and how Kathleen wanted to look. She assumed that they were engaged and went to the back to bring out some dresses that hadn't been put on the rack yet. The saleswoman began talking about what to get, "Let me see, you're about a 8 or 10," she said while sizing Kathleen up. "Right?" Kathleen shrugged her shoulders, because she really did not know. "If you're looking for something for that party, these three would make every eye pop out, Dearie. I wish that I had your figure; because you could wear a cotton sack and look good." Frank was quick to "Amen" her statement. It was uncommon for black people to try on dresses in stores unless they were buying it for sure or for alterations, but the saleslady slipped Kathleen in back and asked her not to come out- she would come back and help her make a choice. She diverted anyone else who wanted to try on a dress to the other side of the store; claiming that there had been some water damage in one of the dressing rooms. Perhaps it was the uniform that Frank was wearing that caused her to go out of her way. All the while she was helping them, the saleslady mentioned that her son had just been drafted, and spoke of her late husband who was an ex-Naval officer in WWII. Patriotism outweighed the racism of the south, and there were always good white people who did not want or let everyone know how nice they could be to Negroes. Whatever the reason, Kathleen quickly tried on this well-fitting red dress, and the saleslady gave her approval. When Frank prepared to pay for it, the saleslady said that it was on sale for half price. The dress had a "for sale" tag on it from the original price of $79.99, but Frank was prepared to pay it, when the sales lady quoted about $40.00. He thanked the lady, but she stopped him and rang it up at the counter saying, "Oh, yes, I forgot to give you the 20% employee discount, now, you go and knock 'em dead, girlie, and you be careful and take good care of your fiance, soldier, you hear?" Kathleen wanted to hug the lady, but refrained, knowing how much trouble that could bring for the both of them. This experience would stay with her forever, for it proved that the heart of some southern white people was not black- as she had seen and been taught, but a lot like the people she had grown up around- Colored people, Negroes-family.

The Fasse's return brought mixed feelings. Teddy had enjoyed his independence through the conversations with Kathleen, and he was anxious to spend more time with her, but he also had mixed feelings about his parents' return. He feared that they would try and put a stop to his and Kathleen's friendship, they would not understand that he was becoming a teenager in the real sense, but with little opportunity and a natural desire to be around the opposite sex, Kathleen would be the answer to most of his problems. They greeted each other with their usual hug, but this time,

Teddy was less childlike-something his father noticed almost immediately. They greeted Kathleen, but Mrs. Fasse told her that they would like to have a minute alone with her after they unpacked. Mrs. Fasse was not one to allow her clothes to remain in a suitcase for very long. Procrastination was a concrete thief of time in her eyes, so Ms. Fasse began putting away the clean clothes and giving Kathleen the dirty ones to be laundered.

Kathleen was not looking forward to this confrontation, as she was certain that they would express their disappointment with Dorothy's visit- or her failure to communicate with them prior to her coming. Whatever the case, Kathleen braced herself. She was used to bad news, and this would be no surprise to her if they told her to leave. Anticipating the worse scenario as usual, Kathleen again reverted to her universal comparisons of white people- only this time she gave the south a positive edge. She thought that there were very few, if any, live-in housekeepers in Memphis with a teen aged son in the home. If Kathleen had the same position back home, she would probably have been accused of hanky-panky between a maid and her young master- especially with their having such a close friendship as she and Teddy had. With the age-old perception of voluptuous black "Jezebel" women- born magnets to the desires of unsuspecting white men-Kathleen would certainly have been categorized as such. The slave mentality of the south dictated as much, with card carrying headlines: **Black Housekeeper In Home-Will Screw The Menfolk!** Kathleen waited in disappointment that that was what Mr. and Mrs. Fasse thought of most black people, too. Later on in the evening they asked Kathleen to come into their bedroom. They carefully shut the door, making sure

119

that Teddy had retired for the evening. They invited her to sit on the brightly patterned loveseat that occupied one corner of their room. While Mr. Fasse was clearing his throat, Kathleen looked around the room, committing the décor to memory. It was impeccably clean and neat, smelling of fresh flowers from the air-freshener they always used in their bathroom. Kathleen planned to use some of Mrs. Fasse's ideas some day when she had her own home; when she had become successful at something. She dreamed of having nice things like the Fasse's had, and even having a maid to take care of them. An eternity seemed to pass before any dialogue began. Just as Mr. Fasse called her name, Kathleen stood and told them that she would quit now before any harsh words were spoken that they all would regret. She expected a cacophony of tongue lashings from them, but instead Mr. Fasse looked at Mrs. Fasse and began what would result in an evening of volleying remarks from each of them. "You will do no such thing, young lady. We won't have it, right, Betty?" He did not give her a chance to respond to his question before he started his next line. "Now, I don't know if you are happy being here with us, but we certainly are happy to have you here-especially Teddy." By this point, they both spoke at a whisper. "You may already know this, but Teddy has been so gravely ill that we didn't know if we would have him with us at all. We're very grateful to God for him, and we know that we indulge him too much-letting him go too far when he speaks to us, or having his way. He says what he wants and get what he asks for. Believe me, we were not raised like that, neither did we raise our daughter that way. But Teddy, well, Teddy's different. While we are lenient with him, we are very, very protective of him. We don't want him to be hurt or disappointed in people. It's very easy to take advantage of someone who is handicapped, so that's why we have gone out of our way to make certain that Teddy knows how to do many things that healthy people do- piano, ham radio, music, the whole shebang. But-we realize that he's getting older- a teenager for goodness sakes, a young man with ... with needs, you understand... and...and...Betty, you can take over now." He had turned as red as a beet and was sweating –in the words of Kathleen's grandmother- "like forty going north." Mrs. Fasse continued, "Well, we know that,...uhm, that sex is on his mind, and... well, we want to be careful that he doesn't look to you for...for, shall we say, sexual options?" Kathleen knew the direction that this was going, and her nose was getting wider with anger by the minute. That dreaded double date with back home, her uncle's lies, the appearance of her doing wrong when she wasn't, pushed its way to the front of her mind. "We want to ask you something, dear. We've noticed how close you and Teddy have become, and well, well... Uhm, uh, would you be offended if... if we asked you to talk with Teddy about the birds and the bees? We know that sooner or later he's going to want to...to experience a woman, but it's so unsettling to us, as his parents, you know; he's so young, yet he probably knows more than we did at his age about... about sex." Kathleen's eyebrows were raised with their comments, along with a feeling of relief. Mr. Fasse continued, "I don't know what the traditions are in the south, but sometimes, Minnie, a Jewish father might, well, shall we say provide their son with a service for his first time with a woman, just so it's controlled and he's protected. My father did, but my mother never knew it or never spoke of it. ' happened a couple of years after my Bar Mitzvah. I was hanging around..." Mrs. Fasse quickly interrupted him with a loud clearing of her throat. "We know that Dorothy's visit was a surprise, and we don't want to make you feel that you can't have any company over. We want you to feel that this is your home, too. We trust you implicitly, and we know that you would do anything to help Teddy. He's developed a crush on you, but I guess you know that." Kathleen tried to interrupt, but Mrs. Fasse spoke louder. "We really don't mind that; we think that's healthy. So we're really asking that you kind of look after him- look for the signs or clues that might indicate that it's time for Teddy to...well, know some things. We would really appreciate your telling us, and doing what you can to help him. All right dear? And if you happen to get a little lonely for male companionship, let me know. We know some nice young men who would love to take you out-Negro men with character. But promise me that you won't ever get mixed up with cab drivers. They are some of the worse crooks you'll ever know." She was about to go on, but Mr. Fasse interrupted her and told her to let Kathleen go to bed. He thanked Kathleen for listening and hoped that they hadn't embarrassed her too much. She smiled, and told them "No", said goodnight and went to her room. After closing her door, she grabbed her mouth, turned around and laughed, and said "Whew." Kathleen thought about how her life and baseball were so much alike- just when she thought someone was about to put her out, there she was- safe, with no runs, no hits and a possible home run with the next swing. What kind of people trusted her that much... and what if they knew that she was Kathleen, now an 18 year-old teenager, not unlike their Teddy, who knew very little about the facts of life? That thought had to go on the backburner, for Minnie had been given a task to talk with Teddy about the birds and the bees, but Kathleen knew less than he did. If the Fasses only knew, she thought, Teddy doesn't need talking to, just talking with or listened to. She recalled the conversation between him and Bernie and their innuendoes about sex. After some thought, Kathleen knew why they asked her- it was the ploy of getting her to remain close and responsible for Teddy, and possibly there would be no violation of the relationship. They would almost be assured that there would be nothing sexual between Teddy and Kathleen. Kathleen smiled as she prepared to shower and go to bed. She didn't think of Teddy that way, and she never would have done anything like that. Now, that may not necessarily be true of Dorothy- but even she was not drawn to jail bait. She would do as they asked, knowing full well that Teddy was going to laugh about it and make a game of it with his parents. Kathleen planned to start the talks the next day, or whenever they found themselves alone; she planned to report to them and keep everybody happy and contented.

Mr. Fasse was not feeling well and stayed home from work the next day. Mrs. Fasse asked Kathleen to go shopping with her, because they were going to have someone over for dinner the next day and wanted to get something special. Kathleen asked who was coming and she told her that it was one of her husband's business associates who had also been a neighbor in the apartment where they used to live. He and his son would be dining with them and she was going to cook their favorite meal. As they got into the car, she explained that he had not long moved back to New York after being in Florida on business, and they were anxious to see them. "I'm going to fix some of my famous lasagna, and I'm ordering a special cake from Waulbaums, with lemon frosting- I heard you say that you liked lemon, Minnie. Would you...would you fix your hair the way you do? You know, straighten it, and put the cluster of curls on top and bangs tomorrow night. I love that style on you. Oh, and you don't have to wear your uniform tomorrow; wear something nice." Mrs. Fasse's mouth was moving almost as fast as the car. She passed Waulbaum's to go to a special Italian store miles away. Kathleen did not know what was up her sleeve, but she knew that Mrs. Fasse was planning something- something that would involve her. She even mentioned purchasing two outfits for Minnie as a gift- one for the dinner and another more formal one that she felt would be appropriate if she ever went to an opening of a play or Broadway. Kathleen, who had left a perfectly good red dress back in Memphis, thought about her reason for buying it and decided to ask Mrs. Fasse why. She answered, "Just in case you might need it one day and you'll have it. I took the liberty to look in your closet and you had no dress or evening wear. Clothes certainly can make the man, but most assuredly makes any woman, Minnie." Kathleen had been thinking back to her first real grown-up dress and what happened when Frank picked her up.

When Frank arrived to pick up Kathleen for the party, he had a corsage. His tux fit perfectly and his shoes shined like a new mirror. He rushed out of the car, jumped over the three steps to the porch, rang the doorbell and waited. When the storm door opened, Dorothy appeared and gave Frank a hug, complimenting him on how well put together he was. "I might have to kill this girl and go with YOU myself," she kidded. He entered, spoke to everyone, sat down and pretended to listen to the small talk from Ms. Clemmie. Frank looked periodically toward the hallway. In what seemed like an eternity, but was actually about five minutes, Kathleen's leg and super spike- heeled shoes became visible. Frank stood up, while following the path of her leg to the rest of her body. He flashed a smile that became progressively wider with each revelation of her body. His bottom lip dropped; he stood there staring like a cement statue without saying a word. He was mesmerized as the knee length fitted blood red dress Kathleen was wearing hugged her every curve. Although Frank didn't realize that the chiffon dress with an underlay of satin looked every bit like a designer's pride- expensive and luxurious looking- and he was fully aware that it would be just another dress without Kathleen in it. She was a woman and wearing this dress, Kathleen felt and acted the part. She had on gold pointed toed shoes and carried a matching clutch purse and small pearl earrings that she borrowed from Dorothy and her Aunt Red. Frank explained that he took the liberty of bringing over a pair of long white evening gloves that belonged to his aunt, if she wanted to wear them. She thanked him and put them on. Frank thought that if there were black queens in Memphis, Kathleen could easily be mistaken for one. Frank's breathing became more rapid with anxiety as he opened the door. He then took her hand escorting Kathleen out to the porch. He seemed to come back from the almost euphoric dream-state he was in to put his head back inside to say, "Good evening" to Ms. Clemmie and the others. He opened the car door for her and then made his way as quickly as possible to the American Legion Hall where the dance was held. Kathleen thought this was an Audrey Hepburn moment-only she was Audrey.

125

Wanting to make an entrance and grab the attention of everyone in the Hall, Frank parked the car, and with Kathleen on his arm, walked slowly into the building. Kathleen smiled and looked around, wiggling her shoulders to the music that the live band was playing. Every eye, male or female, turned toward Kathleen's direction when she walked in the Hall. They were playing a fast number and Kathleen asked Frank if they could get on the floor. He asked her to wait until they had been seated, and then he would go. There was reserved seating for them along with some of his Army buddies and their dates. Gradually, the guys' dates got closer to them, but the ladies eyes looked could have shot daggers as they focused on Kathleen.

Such an attention-getter was not a welcome entry to the circle of friends at the round dinner table. After introductions were made, Frank asked Kathleen to dance. The music was still fast, but was almost over. They did the Pearl High Philly, an extension of the Philly Dog, dances that required a lot of arm and rear movement. Kathleen became oblivious to their attention, as she enjoyed the music. She usually put part of her bottom lip in her mouth when she danced, and did so, which showed how delighted she was to dance. Frank methodically guided her separate free style dance to moves that were more close to him, and the two moved well together. The night was young, but it soon passed by quickly as the Army buddies seemed to fade from the scene; especially the ones who had asked Kathleen to dance. It was as if she had given off some animalistic pheromone that was like a magnate to the men and a push mower for the women. Kathleen continued to dance but found herself a little tipsy after a few sips of the champagne on an empty stomach. Being underage was no problem, since she didn't look like it, but she was not used to drinking and stopped before she became giddier than she already was. The band took a short break, and someone played records until it was time for them to return. When Frank went to the men's room, one of the band members came to the table and asked Kathleen to dance. He had a cigarette in his mouth and wanted to keep it while he danced. She asked him to please put it out and she would dance with him. He mentioned that he was worried that her boyfriend might get angry about the dance, but she assured him that they were just friends and he wouldn't be angry at all. They were swing dancing, something southerners called "Jit"- short for Jitterbug, but not quite as strenuous. With a fitted dress, Kathleen could not have done such. The man lifted her up and spun her around several times. Her hair was in place, but a few of the cluster curls were trying to come down with each turn. When she noticed that hairpins were falling, she stopped dancing, bent over to pick them up and walked toward the table. The pins had little shiny cut glass for decoration that she did not want to lose. The band member misunderstood her walking away as rejection, or ditching him on the floor while everyone was watching. He grabbed her arm whirling her back to him. She asked him to stop, because her hair was becoming undone, but he ignored her; he was slinging her back and forth, when she landed on the floor while yelling for him to stop. Suddenly the band member was grabbed from behind, turned around, and hit with a hard blow that drew blood from his lip. Several of Frank's Army buddies grabbed the man, dusted him off, and took him outside to talk with him. Frank reached down picked Kathleen up and sat her down at a nearby table. Someone spoke to the onlookers and told them everything was all right and to please continue having a good time.

Kathleen let Frank know that she was all right, but she wanted to go to the restroom to freshen up. When she got there, she went into a stall to fix her garter belt and stockings. In a few minutes, two women came in and began talking. For some reason, Kathleen lifted her legs up and held them when they began to talk. "She had no business dancing with him in the first place," one said. The other added, "That dress is tight as Dick's hatband if you ask me, and the heifer probably gave him some to get that dress- I saw it at a store downtown, and it was about a hundred dollars. Frank must have picked her up for a pretty penny. She looks like a first class whore, to me. My boyfriend told me that they had been writing each other while he was overseas, and she promised to give him some no sooner than he got home. She doesn't really know him; ain't never seen him until he got here, girl." The other girl responded with, "You lying?" Then the other girl; continued. "Any woman that would sleep with a man and doesn't really know him is less than a $2 whore." The other girl added, "$1 whore. You know a good whore will at least talk to you before taking your money. Frank is parading her around like she is some...some kinda queen. She' a little flirty heifer, she is, and somebody is going to get hurt from her mess. I bet that's what happened with that man in the band; she probably said something to him to lead him on. Let me get in here and pee, I'm so full that my stomach is about to pop." "Me too," replied the other girl. Kathleen took off her shoes, quietly tipped out of the stall, and noticed that they had left the water running. She washed her hands as they continued to talk. Kathleen wondered why they wanted to rag on her; she had said less than two words to them all night. The girls continued to talk about something that Kathleen was certain that they didn't want anyone else to hear, but she couldn't help but listened carefully and made a sneaky, but hasty exit.

People were still dancing on the floor, as Frank stood at the table waiting until Kathleen got there. She pulled him to the floor and whispered something in his ears. When the other ladies returned, Frank and Kathleen went back to the table with a big smile on their faces. One of the guys mentioned that they were going to pop the question to his girlfriend just before they arrived. "I think I'm going to make an honest woman out of her, man. She has been going it alone for a while now, and she wants to get married. They must have fallen in the toilet, man. Women- they just have to go together, don't they. Being in Nam makes a man think, you know. Coming home to a baby that when you left was an embryo can wake a man up, you know." The ladies came from the restroom and sat down, showing particular attention to their respective men. Kathleen began the conversation. "Hey, you mentioned popping the question why not do it now? This is just as good a time as any; don't you think? And she certainly won't say 'no' with an audience listening." Frank encouraged his buddy as well, while the other young woman and her man chanted "yeah, yeah, come on." The intended fiance asked him not to do so in front of everyone." '... just wait until we're alone"- trying to spite Kathleen for suggesting such. The girl was anxious to make the soldier her husband, but not with Kathleen controlling the proposal. The guy ignored her and asked anyway, hearing an affirmative reply. Everyone applauded and congratulated the couple, when Kathleen began to talk about how wonderful it is to be honest

129

with the man or woman one marries, and commented about the sanctity of marriage. Then she mentioned the baby and asked to see a picture of him. "Well, my goodness, he looks a lot like…like you, and you too"-pointing to the cousin of her fiance who was dateless and sitting near the end of the table. He was not an Army buddy, but a relative who looked out for the girl while his cousin was at war. "Tell me, when you were in the bathroom just now, did you decide to tell your fiancée that little secret you mentioned? I just happened to be in there a few moments ago when you ladies were talking. Shall I tell him what you said?" The girls began perspiring like the water from Niagara Falls when they heard this, and interrupted the conversation immediately. "NO! I…I'll tell him. Uh, could… could I have a word with you for a minute… uh, Kathleen, isn't it?" "Certainly, honey; excuse me, Frank." The ladies went over to the corner and whispered, with Kathleen smiling all the while. "Please, don't tell him, I'm sorry. We…we were just talking because… we uh, are kinda jealous of the attention that our men were giving you and all. When you have a baby, you can't exactly put a dress on like that. Anyway, it's over between me and Ja- I mean, his cousin- and I'm not sure that he's the baby's… da… not really. Please, don't…I really do love Sam, I do. Although Kathleen felt badly, she still felt better having the upper hand. She knew that she would never have told about the possibility of the baby not being Sam's, but she wanted the girls to know who they were talking about and how unfair it was. She related some of these thoughts to the girl, promised not to tell, but wanted and apology from both of them. After returning to the table, things went well. The ladies were civil, and an apology did come even from the "yes" friend. There was still a little tension at the table, but when Kathleen and Frank left the dance, there was a general "at ease" from the others, and a huge sigh of relief from the newly engaged girl. Kathleen was proud of herself for using her head. This was so very much like her mother, she thought. Her mother had always tried to avoid confrontations, but would quickly take on anyone who wronged her children or other members of her family, which could result in a confrontation if need be-and Kathleen was not beyond doing so- just like her mother.

The dance was about over and it was time for the two of them to leave. Kathleen smiled, thanked Frank and kissed him on the cheek, as he opened the passenger side of the car for her to sit. The red tight dress contributed to the regal look Kathleen exuded as the bright street light near them shined directly on her already glowing face. When Frank crossed around to the other side of the car, there was a thud and a scuffle that led Kathleen to scream. A man was almost getting the best of Frank, as Kathleen jumped out of the car to run around the side and help him fight his attacker. She took off her shoes to move faster, raising them up to hit the man when she stared into the eyes of Ernest. He pushed Kathleen down and shouted, "Get the fuck out of the way, ya two-timing bitch." Frank took this opportunity to kick the living daylights out of Ernest with ju jitsu. Kathleen was stunned, but managed to get up and stop Frank from doing any more damage. By this time an audience had gathered, and Frank's friends grabbed both of the men. "You know this man, Kathleen?" She answered slowly, "Yes... yes, he... he was my boyfriend." She stared at Ernest, who was about as drunk as a fish marinated in vodka, and was spotting the front of his pants from getting the piss kicked out of him. He told the men to turn him loose, while the proprietor came out and threatened to call the police if the scene did not break up. Ernest looked at Kathleen and asked her to go with him. She could see that he was unable to drive, so she offered to drive him home. "I can drive with my eyes closed, girl; are you coming with me or not?!" Kathleen looked at him, and at Frank and everyone standing around and told Ernest "No." She begged him to call a cab, but being the bullheaded jealous fool that he was got into his car and drove off. "Sonny, no please!" She had tried to refrain from calling him that, since it was his family's nickname for him-but somehow the name "Sonny" just blurted out of Katheleen's mouth. Frank made the necessary apologies to the crowd, and thanked his friends. The two of them drove off to Kathleen's house, pulled into the driveway and noticed a trail of steady tears that had flowed down her cheeks. Showing himself the gentleman, she wiped her face with his handkerchief and held her in his arms. "You…you're in love with him?" Kathleen answered, "I… I don't know even know what love is." Frank shushed her as she quietly sat up to dry her eyes. The spirit of confession was overpowering and he proceeded to listen to her as she opened up to him. "I'll get the dress cleaned. Thank you, thank you very much. Frank, I… I went out with you because he was ignoring me; he treated me like I wasn't important. 'Now he's acting like he wants me back. I'm confused and… and I'm hurt…and don't know if I want to be with him… and. See, he's… the first- the only man I. I just don't know what to do." Frank was patient and rocked her until she calmed down. Kathleen began to calm down, and she looked up at him. Frank kissed her softly on the lips several times. "A man could fall in love with you very easily, you know. If he feels anything like I do at this moment, then I understand why he acted the way he did. But hell, I didn't do anything to him. I hadn't even kissed you when he came after me. The man is jealous, Kathleen, and you are not helping the situation. If you want him, be with him; if not... then be with...with anybody you want. Don't jerk him around. If you were mine, the Army might have to send somebody to get me because you' make it so damn hard to leave you." He never stopped looking into Kathleen's eyes the whole time he spoke. She felt something, something confusing; something almost forbidden. It was the first time that she had wanted another man to caress her since meeting Ernest. Frank's words were being absorbed not only by her ears but by her heart. Frightened, she slowly loosened herself from him and moved towards the door. She didn't want him to know the effect that he was having on her, so she reached for the door to open it, paused, turned back, looked at him again as he was about to get out and open her door. She touched his arm lightly, and he stopped before getting out. He turned and stared hungrily at Kathllen, as if to devour her would be the most natural thing to do. They kissed, and kissed and she was making sounds that she never had that were more passionate than she had ever experienced. His tongue gently met hers and as the tips of their tongues teased each other, Kathleen's body tingled like little orgasmic fireballs darting her from head to toe. He kissed her neck and planted his mouth on her breast with little or no resistance from Kathleen. She began to moan, he slid his hand under her dress, and she did not resist. He moved it farther and farther up, and her legs opened and their mouths became one with intensity. Then he worked his way to her panties,

133

not forcefully, but rubbing her; Frank put two fingers in his mouth and wet them lubricating them enough to gradually work one finger inside her. She was heated- overheated with desire, ready for lovemaking-wet and moaning. He continued to do this faster while touching her clitoris with each time with another finger. He was skilled, gentle, but slightly rough. Her vulva was swollen with excitement. Kathleen felt things that seemed very natural and satisfying-as her breathing amplified inside the car. Frank skillfully continued to touch her, moving faster and with a rhythm that led her to whisper "don't stop" until she exploded-finally breathing harder and trembling while she held him tight. She even held his hand in place for a moment longer, until her breathing became steadier. She was holding him tightly around the neck with her right arm, and allowing her hand to rest on his hand moving with the rhythm happening under her dress, while looking deeply into his eyes. Suddenly Kathleen trembled and jerked vigorously in a different way- reacting to what she felt was a shameful way for her to act-for any woman to act. Kathleen allowed Frank to see her; feel her have an orgasm-something she had never had with Ernest, and with such abandonment that it made her cry with ecstasy. At the same time she cried with confusion. Kathleen pulled hand away, jumped out of the car, tearing the dress slightly on the seam and hopping the porch steps as fast as her spike heeled legs could carry her. She managed to calm down enough to ring the bell. Frank tried to touch her, but she wouldn't let him. She tried to fix her hair and clothing before someone came to the door. She kept her head down until she was about to go inside. Frank apologized for what he did; and told her not to be ashamed. He took out a handkerchief and wiped the hand that he had used, and told her that he would keep it. "Please, baby, don't feel bad, you didn't do nothing wrong. I'm sorry if I...," he begged. Kathleen couldn't look at him and said nothing as she ran into the house and straight to the bathroom. She turned on the water and put both her hands over her mouth so no one would hear her cry. Ms. Clemmie had let her in, and knocked on the bathroom door asking if she was alright. "I... I ate something that upset my stomach, but I'm fine, Ms. Clemmie; just fine." Kathleen took off her clothes, and looked at herself in the mirror, shook her head disapprovingly, and filled the tub with steaming water. Kathleen sat with steam coming off her body and rocked herself holding her shoulders as tears rolled down her face.

Kathleen was disappointed in herself for many reasons. She drank, and that was not like her. She questioned if she was good enough for any man; the way that she acted with Frank, so shamefully inappropriate. She knew that she could never see him again, but even more, she knew that she had acted like the whores that her grandmother and those girls at the dance talked about. Was it Frank, or would she have acted that way with any man? Was her stepfather right in calling her a whore? The night began with plans to do a friend a favor; make Ernest jealous. An unexpected sensual episode that left her trembling with uncertainty was not in the plan. Kathleen was shocked to know that she could be out of control like that and led solely by her emotions. She was acting like a woman who played games; like when she had played ball as a girl- only this time she had made a big error. She had runs, hits, but the errors meant that there would be no man left; no man waiting at home base. She thought of running again- running fast to safety, but she couldn't answer the question, "Where is home?" Kathleen decided never to be with Frank again, not because of him, but because of fear-fear of what she might do.

That night, dinner was extra special because Mrs. Fasse, in the words of Kathleen's grandmother, "put her foot" in the meal-meaning it was finger licking good. She made certain that Kathleen tasted everything that she made, chicken fricassee, salad with French dressing, asparagus sprouts with hollandaise sauce, a baked potato, wine, and a lemon like tart for dessert. The appetizer was a tray of assorted cheeses that Kathleen was certain had come all the way from every European country on the map- and then some. What was all of this about, she thought? Was Mrs. Fasse getting ready to introduce some nice Jewish boy to her? She knew that interracial relations existed; she had seen Pearl Bailey, Lena Horne, Sammy Davis and Harry Belafonte with spouses of other races and religions. She was not going to be a part of that. Kathleen never knew anybody black in Memphis who did that, and she was not going to be the first.

Teddy told her that he had overheard his parents talking about introducing a man to Minnie, so she wouldn't be lonely. Mrs. Fasse had noticed that from time to time, how quiet Minnie had become and that she stayed home on her day off. She thought it unhealthy for any young woman to do, so she planned this dinner to prevent that. Mrs. Fasse wanted her to have a companion, only it had to be one that they chose to alleviate fear and any possibility of unsavory characters entering Minnie's life.

Dinner was to be at seven-thirty with cocktails and appetizers at seven sharp. The doorbell rang at exactly six fifty seven, as Kathleen looked at the clock in her room. She wondered how she was supposed to work things; how was she to serve and entertain the gentleman who was coming? Mrs. Fasse said that she did not have to do anything, but Kathleen found herself anxious- about the evening. "I'll get it," Mrs. Fasse announced, gesturing for Minnie to stay back in her room until she called her. Mrs. Fasse took Kathleen to Macy's and bought her a very conservatively fitted skirt, blouse and sweater that hugged Minnie's figure. A few minutes after the guests arrived, Mrs. Fasse called, "Minnie, honey, would you come here for a moment? I have someone I want you to meet." She took the time and walked down the hall to the living room where her eyes met one of the most gorgeous men she had ever seen in her life. He extended his hand and she gave him hers. "Lenny, this is our new daughter, housekeeper and friend Minnie. Minnie this is Lenny James." He injected, "The man with two names; if you forget one, I'll answer to the other. 'Nice to meet you, Minnie, but forgive me, you don't look like a Minnie to me. This is my son, Clyde. He hates his name, so please, call him "CD". Somehow young people like to be called initials these days." She shook hands with the boy who was no more than 12 or 13 years old. Everyone followed Mrs. Fasse and the others for cocktails in the living room. Mrs. Fasse whispered to Kathleen to ask him what he would like to drink, and he replied, "Uh, Scotch, on the rocks please. Just as Kathleen prepared to make it, Mrs. Fasse interrupted her, "No, no, not tonight. Mr. Fasse and I will tend bar, right honey? A man of few words, Mr. Fasse nodded his head and said, "Of course, honey." Kathleen sat down in one of the matching chairs while Teddy and CD went back to the room. Kathleen asked if they wanted soda;

Mrs. Fasse handled that too. "I'll bring them something in a few minutes, sit back down and get acquainted with Lenny, Kathleen. He's quite the artist, you know, he does wonderful charcoals and water colors. It's one of his hobbies, but many of them are in galleries." Just then, that perfect recall brain of Kathleen's began working. She remembered seeing various artists on the CBS Sunday morning television show, as well as NBCs Today Show with Dave Garroway. Kathleen was always fascinated with the happenings of New York, London, and Paris and often thought of going to them all. Somehow, being around Lenny was like seeing the two shows all over again, only this was for real. Kathleen asked, "So, you're an artist? Uh, do you paint from memory or imagination, or do people pose for you? He appeared to in a daze when Kathleen spoke to him, but he quickly focused on her crossed legs. When Kathleen repeated her question, he apologized for not paying attention to her, saying that he was preoccupied with concerns at work. However, both Kathleen and Mr. Fasse saw where his eyes were fixed- on Kathleen's smooth, light-skinned hocks- as men from the south called them. "I am an artist like Betty said, but that's a hobby that seems to be rapidly turning into a business. Some people saw my work at an exhibition for amateur artists and bought some. I don't usually prefer models, but lately I've been getting commissioned to do some nudes or abstract portraits. And you, what do you like? I mean do you have any hobbies?" Kathleen told him, "No, but sewing is kind of a hobby. Actually, where I came from, it's a way of saving money. I usually see an expensive outfit in a book, I mean a magazine, and buy the material that's a less expensive and make it. I can draw a little, but I don't really have any hobbies. I do like to ride a bike." He asked, "Yeah, staying in shape...do you have a stationary here?" Kathleen answered, "Huh, oh, no, but Mr. Fasse does; could he use some of yours?" The way both men looked gave away Kathleen's age and lack of sophistication. Kathleen was intuitive enough to know something she said was wrong when Lenny and Mr. Fasse gave a little chuckle. Mr. Fasse explained. "I think that he means, do you ride one of the exercise bikes, I think." Kathleen was flushed that her attempt at adulthood had failed. Suddenly, she did not want any food, any company, any Lenny. She wanted to run again; retreat to her room and not come out for the rest of the evening. She rose to excuse herself, but would not give Lenny the satisfaction of knowing that she cared what he thought. "I like all kind of bikes, the one's that move outside and inside or -stationary. We tend to run back where I came from. Kind of keeps women in shape. It's a southern thing. Would you excuse me for a moment? I want to see if Mrs. Fasse needs any help?"

Kathleen walked slowly into the kitchen, realizing that every move she made was being watched, so she appeared to be in control. 'Make fun of her, will they- she thought! She could tolerate Mr. Fasse, he was older, but he did try to correct her. But Lenny did nothing except snicker, and no woman wants to be laughed at, especially when her ignorance shows. This was the night to play ball, Lenny was up for bat, and Kathleen was going to be the pitcher.

While in the kitchen, Mrs. Fasse kept trying to shush her and moved one of the tendrils of hair that was hanging in front of Kathleen's eye. "Minnie, I think that he likes you. Believe me, dear, I can tell. Now, go back in there and I'm going to call Mr. Fasse in here to help me. I told you, this is my night to cook and serve dinner, and it's your night to be served. You are our guest along with Lenny and his son. She called him with her familiar melodic ring, "Honey, come here a minute, will you?" Kathleen reluctantly went back, passing Mr. Fasse, who almost never smiled, but did so, and gave a thumb's up sign at her. Even though he was what women back home called "a pretty niggah with good hair." Kathleen was determined to pay as little attention to him as possible. Sitting down in the chair nearest him, they began laughing again. "Tell me, did that little misunderstanding about the stationary make you that uncomfortable that you had to leave? Kathleen was shocked at this question, but ignored him, choosing to ask about baseball and who he thought would win the pennant. Information rolled off Lenny's tongue about the Baltimore Orioles, a team Kathleen knew little about, and others. She seemed disinterested, when all of a sudden he stood up and bent down on one knee taking her hand. "I'm truly sorry if I offended you when I laughed. I thought it was cute the way you misunderstood; I didn't think you dumb, maybe ignorant to the northern way of speaking. Obviously, you were affected by that, and there would be no way that I would want a lovely young lady like you to be offended. Please, accept my apology. It's just so refreshing to see a beautiful woman who does not know everything in the world about everything. Believe it or not, a man-well, this man-enjoys a woman that he can teach or talk with about little things as well as business and (he suddenly veered) – you have the beautiful brown eyes that I could get lost in, you know- so don't look at me too much." Kathleen's heart raced, as she could not take her eyes off him. She felt that she had to speak or she would cry just from his charm alone. "I forgive you, but you can get up now." This was a man like no other she had met. He was sophisticated, mature in his approach and different-and oh, goodness, she thought- "was he pretty or what?" Kathleen knew that the Fasse's were going to spring something on her. She thought possibly a Jewish man, one who had money, and liked black women- like the man who married Pearl Bailey. Then they could control who she saw while she lived with them. Kathleen's grandmother always talked about being with a man who likes you more than you like him. "All he needs to do it treat you right, even if he has one eye and only three teeth, that's what a good man will do- anyway, he can buy a glass eye and some good false teeth."

The dinner went well, with all parties laughing and talking about subjects that ranged from politics to polo. When the dessert was served, Kathleen got up to clear the dishes, but Mrs. Fasse would not have it. "I told you, Minnie, you are our guest tonight. Now you two might want to go for a short drive before leaving. Lenny said that she took the words right out of his mouth, and a drive would be nice. He asked Kathleen and she said, "Why not, but I want to be back within half an hour." Mrs. Fasse continued her promotion," The boys are on the ham radio and Mr. Fasse and I will put everything in the dishwasher, won't we dear?" Mr. Fasse opened his mouth, but his wife spoke before he could utter another word. "Go on for about an hour or so, and when you come back I'm sure your son will be ready to go. Kathleen excused herself to the restroom, ran the water in the sink and brushed her teeth. She did not want bad breath, even though she decided that she was not going to let him kiss her no matter how charming he was.

141

Lenny had a Lincoln too, which led her to believe that he made a good living. He drove around near Oceanside, and they got out of the car to walk the beach. Lenny talked her into taking off her shoes, and he rolled his pants legs up and walked bare-foot too. He did not talk about himself much, but was complimentary of Kathleen. He seemed genuinely interested in her, but she felt that she had to ask him something. "Where's Clyde's mother? Are you separated, divorced, or what?" Kathleen was as direct as she could be, without seeming too interested. He explained that they had been divorced since their son was two, and she had remarried. She was from a fine Jewish/British home, and their marriage was one of convenience-he converted and she was homosexual. Clyde just happened on a night when they both were cold enough to share a bed together. Lenny got custodial custody, but they both agreed to share in Clyde's care. She got to live with her "roommate" which worked well for both. Lenny moved on to another conversation almost immediately, as he picked up a shell and gave it to Kathleen, then hugged her, thanking her for a lovely evening. He looked her in the eye, bent down and kissed her, which Kathleen expected, but on the forehead, something she did not expect; they went back to the car. Kathleen was a bit disappointed, because she knew that he wanted to do more. She checked her breath, but that was not it. He said little until he got back to the apartment building. He took her hand, kissed it and asked if he could call her. She said yes, and he walked around and opened the door. The trip in the elevator was quiet even though he smiled each time their eyes fell on each other. When they got to the apartment, he held his hand out for her key and opened the door. His son was waiting for him and began what seemed like a ritual by shaking Teddy's and Mr. Fasse's hand, kissing Mrs. Fasse on the cheek, nodding at Minnie, and saying "Shalom; 'see you at Temple." They all said "Shalom" and waved as he closed the door. The Fasse's then looked at her, smiled and waited with baited breath for Kathleen to say something about the evening. Minnie finally spoke, "I'm tired, and if you all don't mind, I'd like to go to bed now. Thank you for this evening; thank you both very much."

Kathleen smiled as she went into her room; knowing that the Fasses were on the edge of their seat to know where she and Lenny went, and if they got along. Kathleen felt the satisfaction of knowing that although her employers controlled the evening, she controlled whether she'd talk about it or not. Kathleen thought about the nice evening she had with the handpicked man, a black Jew, and she wanted to see him again. He seemed interested in her, but did not really make a real pass. He fit the bill of the baseball player who was confident that he could hit a homerun when he got ready, but he didn't know that she, Kathleen, had learned how to punch a hitch in a man's get along- when he teased her enough to get her interest. Game was on. Deep within, Kathleen was glad that the Fasse's introduced her to this interesting, well-to-do, tall, and as Shug would say, "pretty ass" BLACK JEW! She couldn't wait for Dorothy to meet him and size him up.

The night was a hit, she thought, with one classy player waiting at bat. Kathleen thought he hit the ball in a way to let her walk, but it would be a steady walk; and toward home.

CHAPTER IV

You're Out!

Three days after the dinner party, the phone rang and Kathleen answered, "Hello, Fasse residence?" The male voice on the other end of the receiver was not quite legible, as static was heard at 'hello'. "Call back, please," Kathleen yelled, "I can't understand you." The phone rang almost immediately after she hung up; this hello was static free. "Hello, I can hear you, now." The voice on the other end replied, "I'm glad you can, but I'm surprised that you didn't hear me calling your name in my dreams." That deep based voice was familiar, but she wasn't certain who it was. "Hel...lo? Who is this?" The voice replied, "How soon we forget. It's me, baby, Ernest." Kathleen's heart raced, as a large lump entered her throat. She couldn't swallow, she couldn't speak; her knees were weak. "Ernest? Why 'you calling me? I...you said that it was all over between us." She had to sit down; she was trembling and holding her chest. His answer was a series of swiftly thrown questions - "Do you miss me? When are you coming home? Can't a man make a mistake without a woman going thousands of miles away?" Kathleen wanted to jump through the phone. She wasn't sure why, except he evidently missed her and wanted her back. She closed her door and told him to call her Minnie whenever he called. "I'll tell why later on, but...but who said it was all over? Not me. I'm trying to get on with my life, and unless you have something permanent to talk about, I have to go." She pushed the button, and wondered what the hell she had just done. Kathleen was confused because, she wanted to see Ernest just as much as she didn't want to see him. Allowing Ernest back into her life now would be like walking backwards on a tightrope- not only does one not see where they're going, but there might not be enough rope to make her destination. The knight in shining armor feeling was still in Kathleen's mind, so hanging up the phone would either draw him or drive him away. Either way, Kathleen knew that she deserved to be courted, and to be the prize he won. She had never really thought of herself as a prize, but it seemed that the more men Kathleen met the more she realized that she was somebody that someone wanted. An even bigger cloud of confusion was resting inside Kathleen. Because Ernest had known her in the biblical sense, she felt that this man should be her husband. Suddenly Kathleen panicked and thought, "What was I thinking of- hanging up on this man?" She wondered if he would call back and if so, what would she say? What about Lenny? Would Ernest call like he said he would, and what about Frank? Was the man who made Kathleen feel so out of control and like a princess, too, all in the same night- was he alright? Was he alive over in Vietnam? Men confused her. Kathleen thought about Frank even more than Ernest, and every time she did, her body would automatically react. She relived that night with him in the car many times and how she almost gave herself to him. Frank taught her that she could be treated like royalty, and feel real downright passion from the top to bottom. Kathleen wanted to talk with Mrs. Fasse; it mattered to her if Mrs. Fasse thought her to be promiscuous. She wanted to talk with Dorothy, but Dorothy was very busy with something she was doing for her employers.

Kathleen felt uncomfortable concerning her sexual feelings. She tried to discard them like trash, but could not. She had three men on her mind, and fantasized what it would be like sleeping with each one of them, and thought herself a closet whore. Why were all three of these men appealing to her- and vice versa? Wasn't a girl supposed to think about one and one only? Isn't that what she had learned from the movies? God knew her feelings, and she was afraid of what He would do to her for feeling this way.

Kathleen needed God, she thought, because ever since her mother died, she seemed to move away from Him; somehow blaming Him for what happened to her mother, but afraid to admit it out loud. Service to God, she thought might be the only way to keep her from being a whore, but living with Jews would never put her in contact with a church. She thought, maybe Lenny could take her with him to Temple. Maybe there she could find God again, and maybe God could comfort and protect her from herself- and men. Kathleen decided to pray and try to stop thinking so much about her needs.

Teddy had not been feeling well and needed attention, so Kathleen needed to put all her energies into his getting better. Some days, he just seemed more tired than others, and had to rest that concerned Kathleen. Teddy explained

that that was one of the side effects of having had the injury-
he was prone to anemia and fatigue. Iron tablets and clear
chicken soup broth for two or three days, and Teddy would
be his old self again.

It was Monday, and Teddy and Mrs. Fasse were going
to the doctor. His annual checkup for his eyes was overdue,
and Teddy hated going to the doctor's office. Lately, it seemed
that no one was able to get him to go except Kathleen. Teddy
was like a little brother, who had a crush on his sister and
could do nothing about it. Kathleen knew this, and respected
his feelings, but still she also saw that Teddy would just
downplay any medical problem, so he said anything to placate
Kathleen when she asked how he felt. She wanted Teddy to
trust her with everything, as Kathleen did him. She had
even told him her real name and the circumstances that led
her to do so. Teddy proved himself trustworthy. Now that
she was entertaining the idea of getting back with Ernest,
Teddy might turn on her. That, most "don't trust no white
people" advice started playing in Kathleen's head. She knew
for certain that Teddy would not want her to leave, especially
not for a guy who had treated her as shabbily as Ernest had.

"Minnie, you have got to get your license, so you can take
Teddy out sometimes and I can stay at home. He is spoiled
rotten and wants you to go with us to the doctor's. One
would think you two are brother and sister the way you act."
Mrs. Fasse interrupted her train of thought for a moment
by asking, "Who was that on the phone, dear; was it Lenny?
Never mind, that's none of my business. 'Just being nosey- but
I bet it was. I'd like for you go with us today, because Mr.
Fasse isn't feeling well and wants to stay in bed. After we get

back, I'm going to make him go to the doctor, too, if he isn't any better. I don't want to deal with a cross Teddy alone." Kathleen knew Mrs. Fasse like the back of her hand. She was really telling Kathleen that she did not want to leave her in the house with Mr. Fasse. It was common knowledge among southern black people that white men would try to bed their black help if the opportunity arose. Whether this was true in the north was not debatable- "A mane (man) is a mane no matter what color he is"-was frequently quoted by Kathleen's grandmother. Kathleen added, "Give me a minute to change clothes. I really don't want to wear this uniform, if you don't mind, Ms. Fasse." Teddy lit up like the sun. The ride in the car to the doctor's office was a quiet one as Kathleen thought about the last time she saw Ernest; the last time she thought that she would ever hear from him.

"I don't know what to do, Dorothy. I know I hurt Ernest, maybe I should call him-it's been almost five days now and I haven't heard from him." Dorothy's responded with, "Good riddance to trash; he wasn't shit then and he ain't shit now. If I had your face, I wouldn't give a damn about what a niggah thought or felt. Really, I don't give too much of a damn now with the one I got." Kathleen was surprised; she had never really heard Shug talk in a negative way about herself. "There is nothing wrong with your face, Shug, what are you talking about? You got men coming at you like 40 going north. You have a great figure and you're fun. Don't talk about yourself like that." Dorothy was sitting on the porch swing while Kathleen sat on the porch steps. Dorothy stopped swinging and joined her on the concrete steps. "Look, if you want to see the guy, don't let what I say stop you, but you don't know too much about men, Katy. You think that you owe something to Sonny just because he was the first mane to test your poontang. That's the wrong reason to want to be with somebody. Take for instance that Frank. Shit-ittt, now there's somebody who would probably treat you right, but you won't give him the time of day. Aw shit, what am I talking about; I still want that fool I was seeing even after his wife kicked my ass. But that's another story. I guess what I am saying is, if you really want to find out if you and Sonny have a real thang, then you might have to contact him. After that jealous shit he pulled, well, he might have changed his mind about you. Either way, girl, I'm on your side. If you want to see him, I will go with you. I mean, I don't want the niggah trying to whip your ass or nothing. I don't want to have to cut him 'bout 'cha." They both laughed as they hugged each other. Kathleen decided to call him as soon as he got off work. She had to try and patch things up; explain what happened before too much time lapsed.

Ernest did not want to talk on the phone. He asked her to be ready about eight that night, and he would pick her up. She agreed. There was an unusual calmness in his voice as she spoke to him-a calmness that she had never heard before. When he got to the house, he blew his horn and she came running to the door. Just as she was about to open it, Ms. Clemmie called her. "Kathleen, I try to stay out of your business, but child you watch yourself. I 'been hearing about how you and Ernest been at odds, and I don't want anything to happen to you. You remember, this man think he 'been scorned, and he' jealous, and older than you. Now, you be on your guard, you hear me? Do you have money to call us?" Kathleen answered, "Yes, ma'am, Ms. Clemmie, but he ain't going to hurt me; don't worry." Ms. Clemmie added, "I just want you to know, we will send somebody to get you. I heard about the dance you went to and all. Now, Frank wanted to see you before he left, but he brought this here letter for you just in case he didn't. Here it is. Just call us if you need us." Kathleen hugged Ms. Clemmie, put the letter in her bag, and went back to the door.

Ernest pulled up and blew his horn, then got out of the car and stood in the driveway near the porch until Kathleen came to the car. Opening the door for her, he lit a cigarette when he got in, letting the window down, as the breeze blew through Kathleen's hair. She felt uneasy, but she didn't really know why. Ernest was saying nothing, but at every red light he kept staring at her then at the street. She could not figure him out, but she felt uncomfortable and happy at the same time-she was with him again and they were not arguing.

After a twenty or thirty minute ride, it occurred to Kathleen that not only had one word not been spoken between them, but they were now sitting in front of a motel, somewhere on the outskirts of town. Ernest looked at her and asked her if this was all right and she nodded. It really wasn't all right, for Kathleen felt that Ernest had no intention of sleeping with her after the incident with Frank. After all, she thought, there was no commitment between them, except steady bedding with no mention of a ring being placed on her finger. He was not her fiancé; so he had no claim to her. If nothing else, by this time Kathleen had gained some confidence in her own sexuality. She didn't do weird exotic or erotic things like oral sex, but Kathleen had the ability to be that "bitch on a sheet, angel on her feet" type of woman. She knew men enjoyed looking at her and even women complimented her on her legs or her skin. Maybe this was why Ernest looked at her like he did, because whenever they made love, he stroked and rubbed her skin for long periods of time.

Kathleen got out of the car and walked into a small restaurant that was inside the motel. They were somewhere near Mississippi, but she did not know where. They ordered burgers, fries, cokes, and ate in almost solemn silence as Ernest continued to stare at her. Suddenly after the meal was almost finished, he asked her if she had any money, and she said no. "Well, how are you going to pay for your food?" He asked. "Pay for…? You brought me here and asked me to… what' you mean, pay for my food?" Kathleen felt frightened. Ernest continued, "Well, that's what FRIENDS do, they go Dutch for lunch or dinner or they find out if their friend is going to pay for it or not; that's what WE are, right? Friends? " He took out some and paid for his meal, stood up, smirked and walked to the door saying nothing. Kathleen could not believe her eyes. She only had a few dollars in case she needed it, but it was still not quite enough. Kathleen needed seventy-three more cents to pay for the meal. Watching Ernest leave as he did, not knowing where she was or how she'd get home brought an immediate flow of tears. He left her without a word and drove off. No matter what, Ernest would never get a chance to do this to her again ever-she thought. That was the reason for the stare; he planned to hurt her for what she had done. But not this; not leaving her in a place that she had never been; without any money or anything! She looked toward the manager and asked the waiter to have him come to her table. She was going to flash those brown eyes and ask if she could wash the dishes. Kathleen had seen

151

enough Ginger Rogers and Andy Hardy movies to know that a pretty girl could get almost anything, even though since becoming a teenager she had shied away from this kind of cheap philosophy. When the manager came over to the table, Kathleen opened her purse, preparing to tell him about her plight, but found, folded in the corner of the small zippered area a twenty dollar bill. Kathleen had not looked, but remembered that Ms. Clemmie had given her the purse, and was zipping it up as he handed it to her. Kathleen was so grateful that she continued to cry. She was about to hand him the money when he informed her, "Ma'am, the gentleman paid the check before he left." Kathleen did not know what to feel or to say. What kind of trick was Ernest playing? Why did he leave the way that he did? She realized that she really didn't know what kind of man she was dealing with. She asked the manager to call her a cab. She hoped that old Mr. Taylor was available, so she gave him the special cab number to call. Again, the manager spoke, "Ma'am, I don't think that you will need that cab, the gentlemen who came in here with you is out front, and he asked me to tell you to come outside to his car when you' finished." Kathleen walked over to the window and saw him smoking a cigarette and staring into the restaurant. Kathleen thought, "What kind of game was Ernest playing?" She went outside and stood for a moment as he stared and smirked at her; she went back inside to see if she could find a man who was eating alone- anyone other than Ernest to take her back home. She was not going to let him control her, so Kathleen walked over to a man of about 65 and asked if he would take her home, and that she would pay him. She explained that she was was stranded. He was only too happy to comply, and had the rest of his dinner put in a carry-out. Kathleen was a bit nervous and afraid, but she figured that she could handle an old man if she need be. Ernest looked surprised as Kathleen walked out with the old man, but would say nothing to her. He simply got in the car and drove off in the opposite direction.

The man's name was Randy, and he drove her straight home with little conversation. He said that he was married and understood how lovers can have a misunderstanding. Kathleen offered to pay him, but he declined. Just before she got to the stairs, Ernest quickly pulled with screeching tires, got out of his car, stood in the driveway with a cigarette, and stared at Kathleen. He grabbed her and lifted her off the ground, kissing her with a roughness reminiscent of a football tackle. He opened the door and put her in with no resistance on her part; he then drove off to a nearby dark area near an abandoned house and got in the back seat of the car. He pulled Kathleen to the back as she resisted with a light scream. He began to kiss her like a mad man, snatching her underwear off and sucking on her breast through her clothing. Kathleen was both excited and afraid, even though he was hurting her. He was commanding and almost scary in the way he sounded; the way he acted, but Kathleen somehow knew that Ernest was not going to hit her. He pulled down his pants and entered her roughly, without a rubber. Although it was somewhat painful, Kathleen was wildly excited like never before- the only other time she felt like this was with Frank-almost like an animal. Kathleen was loving every minute of it; moaning and groaning, she held him as tightly as he did her. At that very moment of pleasure, she didn't care about anything except what her body was feeling. So this was the point that she had heard talk

153

about- in baseball, when the ball has been pitched and a high pop fly is hit by the batter- you don't know where it's going, but it's exciting to watch it go. This must be what it feels like to fly over the fence to-THE POINT OF NO RETURN- a real home run. Kathleen had two orgasms that made her toes curl and she was as loud as possible. She wondered why Ernest had not done this before, and the thought of getting caught just added to her satisfaction. When Ernest finished, he bit her on the neck, discarded the rubber, and took Kathleen back to the house. Out of breath and sweating, minutes passed before a word was spoken between them. He then lit a cigarette, knowing Kathleen hated the smoke.

Ernest looked at her pulled her close to him and held her tightly, kissing her long and hard on the head. He slid down to her ear and whispered, "This is it, baby. No matter how good it was, this is it. I know that's probably what you did with that guy that night. I always thought that you had some freaky shit in you. No self-respecting girl would screw a man in a car… You-ain't-who- I-thought you-was. He let her go while reaching over her to open the car door. The reason I wanted us to cool off was to see how I really felt about you and see what you would do. My friends tried to tell me. You hanging with your boon coon Dorothy, you were probably a little weird, but I didn't want to listen to them. I guess you showed me, and proved them right. I can't… I wouldn't marry no woman like that. I don't know what the hell you would do the minute we got into a little disagreement. You free now to fuck anybody you want, since that's all you good for…and you are good." Kathleen looked at him and frowned. She was not really sitting there, disheveled, sexually satisfied, and hearing this terrible declaration, this news from the man she thought that she loved and loved her. This must be a dream, because no man would do this to a woman that he cared for, or so Kathleen thought. After a few moments of silence, the South Memphis rage began to stir within her. Kathleen got out of the car, but not before hitting Ernest hard with her fist. She knew that she had been used worse than an old horse ready for the glue factory. If she wasn't a whore, she certainly felt like one now. How could he, she thought, how could he have done this? What was the business at the restaurant? It was like sticking pins deep into her and pushing them deeper and deeper. Kathleen felt like shit. Worse than that, she thought herself to be worse than shit. Kathleen wanted to run, to get away, way away from Ernest or any other man.

The next day she told Dorothy what happened, and they planned the trip to New York. Kathleen had sat in the tub and cried that night until her face turned bright red and her nose began to bleed. She hated herself and she hated all men. At that moment, if she had not liked men, Kathleen thought that she would have easily become a dyke, a bulldagger, making her Uncle's lie and her Grandmother's accusation true. That night made Kathleen want to run away from anything that remotely looked like a man.

Ms. Clemmie noticed her unhappiness after looking at Kathleen for the next two mornings. She barely got out of bed or put on any clothing. Always the one to clean and scrub, she neither ate nor drank anything for two days. She didn't comb her hair or brush her teeth. She had become the poster child for depressed and scorned women everywhere. Dorothy told Ms. Clemmie some of the details leading to the break-up, but could not tell her everything. Ms. Clemmie tried talking with Kathleen, but it was as if she was in a catatonic state. She would occasionally smile, but on the third day, she ate a few bites of oatmeal, sat near Ms. Clemmie on the sofa, collapsed into her arms and cried. Ms. Clemmie told her to call her grandmother, and tell her, reminding her that she was a woman too, and she would understand. Kathleen called, but declined to tell her anything. She heard her Grandmother's voice on the other end asking "Who is this?" Kathleen was silent and hung the phone up gently. She and Dorothy left Memphis- the place where Elvis lived, the place where her mother died, and the place where she was considered "not good enough" to be loved or to be somebody's wife; just a whore. She was ready to exit Memphis for Timbuktu, Russia, or anywhere; anywhere far away from the bluff city and as far, far away from Ernest as she could get.

CHAPTER V

The Bases Are Loaded

Kathleen did the wash, put all the clothes away, prepared the swordfish for dinner, and had the whole apartment shining by day's end. She was going to pack a few things and stay over Dorothy's house, and Lenny promised to drive her after dinner. Dorothy was invited to have dinner with Kathleen and Lenny the week before, and they seemed to get along better than Kathleen expected. This was certainly unusual, since Dorothy, as a rule, did not particularly go for pretty men. Lenny was an exception to the rule. Normally, Kathleen would not have accepted the invitation, but Lenny called persistently since the twenty-six days before of their introduction, the Fasses asked about him for about 20 of them. Shug, Kathleen, and Lennie were supposed to meet at an amusement park, so it really didn't seem like a date with the three of them, but just a fun outing among friends. Teddy seemed jealous during this period; Kathleen was his girl and Lenny was taking her away. True, Teddy had grown accustomed to Kathleen-to their conversations, which were filled with laughter. Even though he could not see Kathleen,

157

Teddy's feelings about her were a testament of how people should feel about each other- seeing with their hearts and not their eyes. Kathleen was older than Teddy, and that bothered him. Teddy felt that if he were older or at least equal to Kathleen in years, he might have a chance-even though he was a Jew. "If Sammy Davis Jr. really knew what he did for people, besides entertain them, he would jump for joy," Teddy would say from time to time. Kathleen knew what he meant, but she did not entertain the thought of Teddy as a love interest. He was like a brother, and she could only love him like a sister should.

Teddy asked, "When Lenny gets here, would you tell him that I would like to see him for a minute, please? His voice was assertive, almost father-like. What he wanted to talk to Lenny about was obviously about Kathleen, but she did not dare ask. Lenny arrived promptly, and Kathleen escorted him to Teddy's room. Kathleen looked at her watch. The two spent all of seven minutes together, when Lenny emerged ready with a kind of fake smile. This was hard to discern since Lenny always smiled. They said their proper goodbyes and left. On the way, Lenny said little to Kathleen, so she began the conversation. "It must have been quite a conversation you had with Teddy to make you this quiet. Usually, you talk so much when you call me that I hardly get a word in edgewise; is anything wrong?" Lenny asked if she'd mind his could pull over to a little carhop place and get a soda, and Kathleen said, "Yes." "Can we talk frankly without your getting…getting defensive, because if we can't, I might as well take you straight to your destination?" Kathleen answered, "Yes," and waited while he got out of the car; he lit a cigarette. "I forget sometimes that things have not changed; that I am a grown man who can be treated like a boy at the whim of ...of a boy whose pigmentation says he is white no matter if he eats locks and gefilte fish or not." Lenny seemed angry, and to Kathleen he was revealing a side of himself reminiscent of Ernest. "I guess you would understand this even better than I, coming from down south. Where does his little white ass get off trying to tell me what to do? They all think that they can, no matter what their age!" Kathleen asked him what the problem was, and he looked at her as if she should have known and pointed his finger at her and said, "Your young massa' ordered me to leave you alone if I just wanted someone to go to bed with, because he was not going to stand by and let any man hurt you. I asked the upstart if he wanted you and he said, "Who wouldn't, but I know that I am too young, NOW." But if you stayed with them until he was 18, he would probably ask you to marry him. He even mentioned that his hero was Sammy Davis Jr.-whatever the hell that meant. I probably could have swallowed that except I got to thinking. He's a little snot-nosed boy, and I am a full grown ass man. Who does he think he is telling me what to do? If I was not on the color wheel as black, I wouldn't have done that! But they all think that they can... that they have the right to speak to you like you're a slave. That's what I'm mad about! It's like... like no matter how much education you get, no matter where you go, you still just a niggah... just a niggah!" Kathleen said in a soft-spoken voice, "It don't matter what they think-it matters what they do. They don't know how to think any other way. What would make white people sensitive to what you think, unless they walk in your shoes? Isn't that why people have been having all this freedom fighting and voting meetings? They try and make people understand us; 'give us the same respect as white people have always had? You think that I don't know that I'm some black girl from the south who lives in the house with rich, white people who just happen to be Jews? Before I came here, all I knew was how I was supposed to act around white people, because I was taught that from a baby. When I got here, these people did not act quite like the ones where I came from. They... they made me feel grateful and maybe equal in a way- even though I clean their house and they call me their housekeeper. I watched them tell their other Jew friends not to call me *girl*, when that's what they all call their help. I watched Mrs. Fasse treat me like her daughter; concerned about who I am seeing, if I'm comfortable, and have everything I need and some of the things that I want." Lenny injected, "That's just to keep you under their control." Kathleen responded immediately, "Every time someone tried to control what I do that I can remember, none of them were white. One control ain't no better than the other- it just seems worse when it comes from a certain shade of people. Let me ask you something. IF you were an Indian, would it bother you if somebody named a baseball team after you like- The Redskins?" Lenny answered, "Probably not, but..." Kathleen continued, "Why not? You believe yourself to be sensitive to other races, don't you? Then why would you stand for a sports team to be called The Redskins, or the Braves or maybe even the Pow Wows? What if they called them the Jigs, Niggahs, Coloreds? See- it would probably bother a real American Indian person to be called Redskin, even though people may not mean anything by it. Maybe...maybe Teddy didn't mean to hurt your feelings, just protect mine.

He wasn't coming at you like a white boy to a black man- just a boy with a big ole crush, and he's just smelling hisself,' as my grandmother used to say. Could it be possible that what he feels for me is more important to him than your feeling less than a man? Don't get so mad with him about the color of his skin, he didn't make himself. I hate to admit this, but most of the bad treatment I have received has been from (picking up the loose skin on her hand and face) folk like you and me." Lenny stopped and looked at her for a moment as he stepped on his cigarette. He asked her how she got so to be so smart at such a young age. Maybe he was taking what Teddy said too personal. He realized that he was much older than Minnie, but not necessarily more mature.

They walked for a little while longer with Lenny's arm around her neck like a buddy. He told Minnie how much he liked her. Her innocence, her honesty, and her common sense attitude, and how she spoke her mind. He complimented her on her being able to work with her hands, and encouraged her to get the rest of her education. He reveled in telling her about New York's ambiance, and she was eating it up like candy. Lenny was over complimentary about her good looks, but told her that it might end up being a liability in the long run. "How could good looks be a liability, Lenny? I never heard of that in my life-not that I think I'm better looking than other woman. Lenny had walked to the car by this time, leaned against it, crossing his arms and feet. He smiled at her, and took her in his arms. Kathleen let him kiss her. She didn't like it. She didn't like the taste of the *Herbert Terryton* cigarette on his tongue, which he was trying to travel down her throat. She pulled away and spat. "I'm sorry I don't really like the taste of cigarettes. And since you say you like honesty, where in the world did you learn to kiss?" Thinking that she was complimenting him, he said wait until he chewed some gum and he'd try again. "NO," he yelled. "This may be the way ya'll kiss in New York, but we don't kiss like that in Memphis. You don't try to choke a girl with your tongue. You are supposed to be soft and easy, and if it gets rough it's not supposed to make you gag." Lenny looked at her with a frown, said nothing, and walked back to the car. She followed him and apologized for it appeared that Kathleen had hurt his feelings. He opened the door for her and smirked, "That little asshole! 'Know what he told me? He said that he'd really like to be with you and that you liked me. Right afterwards, he warned me about my intentions about you. He said that he had a few tips that would help me get on your good side; you told him that you liked guys who smoked and kissed by ramming their tongue down your throat. I have never felt so damn stupid! How could I have believed he'd tell me the truth?"

Kathleen was almost angry, but after looking at each other, they both laughed. "Snowed by a Jew; maybe there's some truth to the rumor after all," Lenny quipped. "What rumor?" Kathleen asked. "The one about Jews being...rich, not all of them are, but when they're rich, they're very rich. Land; they run the film industry; Broadway. They're top lawyers and business people, unlike a lot of us or REAL white people. That's why I became one. Haven't you ever heard about that down south?" Kathleen wanted to lie, but here she was again-not a sophisticated southern girl- and right in front of Lenny. This time, she defended herself. "Back home, we don't have time to...I have heard of people getting a Jew lawyer, because they say they're the best. I don't know that, and I don't really want to know. I saw and heard enough prejudicial things about black people that I know are not true. Probably many of the things I have heard about Jews are not true either. All I know is how smart are YOU to listen to a teen-aged boy? You're the man; not him. The next time you want to kiss me, ask me; I'll tell you. Can we go now? I have a lot to do tomorrow? Oh, could I have a piece of that gum, please? " Lenny stared at her and smiled, "You're a lot brighter than I thought… not your skin bright… I was talking about"."I know what you' talking about, Lenny; let's go. Dorothy's waiting," Kathleen injected, and said under her breath "check and check mate."

When they reached Dorothy, nothing else about Teddy was spoken. They rode the Ferris wheel, ate cotton candy and had fun; then Lenny drove the girls back to Dorothy's place. He promised to pick her up the next day and take her back. That night, Kathleen told Dorothy about what happened, but Dorothy did not want to talk about it.

Dorothy was gearing up for a conversation with someone, and said she'd talk about it tomorrow. Disappointed, Kathleen thought about the conversation, what Teddy had done, how she missed Memphis, but realized that she was becoming more and more comfortable with herself, and with other people who knew so much more than she did, and she was becoming less and less dependent on any advice from Shug.

When she arrived back at the apartment the next morning, there was a note on Kathleen's phone that Mrs. Fasse stuck with a piece of tape- ERNEST CALLED AND SAID, PLEASE, CALL HIM BACK- COLLECT- NO

MATTER HOW LATE. Her heart beat a little faster. She walked slowly away from the phone, looked in the mirror, walked back to the phone, took the message and threw it in the wastebasket. She would not do it to herself. She was still healing, and vowed to stick it out in New York- no matter what.

It was difficult for Kathleen. Her family, Ernest and Lenny, were occupying spaces and places in her mind and her heart. She missed the smell of Memphis, and Kathleeen wondered if anything had changed- if anyone really missed her, too. She ran back to the wastebasket and pieced together the half-torn note about Ernest. Kathleen picked up the phone and dialed collect, and he accepted. "Hey baby, two words- come home; I miss you." Kathleen opened her mouth, not knowing what she was going to say and blurted, "That's five words. I want to get married, Ernest, and you called me a whore…I'm not a whore. I'm not coming home…ever." There was silence, and just as she was about to put the receiver down he said, "Then come home, and I'll give you what you want. I'm sorry, baby." Kathleen had a huge smile on her face, but would not let her voice indicate how she felt. The game was winding up, there were two men left on base, and one just hit a home run, while another had fouled. Kathleen was now the umpire in the game, and she was in control of the outcome.

CHAPTER VI

Another Foul

They had been so wonderful to Minnie. If the Fasses knew that Minnie liked something, the Fasses would surprise her with the best ways of enjoying it: a special radio with an earplug so that she could hear the World Series, a small stereo system so that she could play her favorite records, and albums by artists that they liked-Nina Simone, Tony Bennett, Judy Garland, Nat King Cole, Della Reese, Sam Cooke, Brook Benton, Frank Sinatra, and Dionne Warwick. Mrs. Fasse would bring home costume jewelry for her like matching earrings, bracelets and necklaces, along with handkerchiefs that were monogrammed. She schooled the housekeeper about the Jewish customs, holidays, pumpernickel, gefilte fish, and how retail was not necessarily a bad thing, but to avoid it if one could. Kathleen thought that she was becoming a little spoiled, and wondered how she could ever leave them- especially Teddy. He had become her best friend and confidant; and she was his. They both laughed about things that only the two of them understood. Kathleen knew that Teddy was going to be devastated after she left, so she felt that she had to tell him, if no one else.

Two days had passed since Ernest proposed, of sorts, and Kathleen had decided that she would leave after the next pay period, two weeks away. When she told Ernest, he protested, wanting her to pack and leave immediately. At present, he said that he could not afford for her to get the bus, so she figured that she would wait until she had saved the money to leave. This revelation of Ernest's lack of enthusiasm concerning her way home sent signals that Kathleen chose to ignore. Kathleen had become quite frugal, because Mrs. Fasse provided most of the things that she wanted. Dorothy's employers, trendsetters and socialites, gave her clothes that fit both she and Kathleen. The social column of the local Long Island news described Dorothy's employers as people who hardly wore an outfit more than once- but if one counted over-seas trips, they may have worn them four or five times- so the clothes looked fairly new, and they were expensive. She called Dorothy to give her the news, but deep down she wanted Dorothy's opinion on her decision to leave. "Are you out of your ever-loving mind, girl? He is playing you like a fiddle! And you are going to pay for the privilege to get back home to him? Girl, you need a pill, a needle stuck up your ass and quick!" Dorothy went off on her like never before. Kathleen's deeper conscience knew that if Ernest really wanted her home, he could drive to New York, for this man had driven miles to see a ballgame, to visit family members, purchase a certain style of clothes or shoes- or just to get away with his friends. Why wouldn't he come up to New York, if he wanted to see her? Her explanation to Dorothy was met with deaf ears- "See, Shug, he is going to send for me, but he can't really afford it now. I thought that if I meet him halfway, it would speed up our seeing each other." Kathleen could not believe herself at this point, but she thought it was the right thing to do. Dorothy told her to think about it overnight and talk it over with Mrs. Fasse. Kathleen thought- Dorothy would have done the exact same thing, if that married man wanted her to come home. But something was different-the object of Shug's desire had changed, and Kathleen noticed it the last few times they were together. She knew that Dorothy was having fun with someone, possibly someone who visited the house, and that man from Memphis was temporarily out of her mind. The idea of going back to Memphis almost never came up in their conversation- just sex and money.

A few days later after breakfast, Mr. Fasse and Teddy went for a ride. This was the day Mrs. Fasse set aside to show Kathleen some traditional Jewish recipes and explain customs related to Jewish holidays like Passover, Yom Kippur, and Chanukah. It was as if Mrs. Fasse had planned on Kathleen becoming Jewish. Kathleen thought maybe that's why she wanted Lenny to date her, and telling her these things would help her to be a better prospect for marriage. She was always hinting at things like that. Lenny may have been cute, but he was not really Kathleen's type. He was older than most men she had would have dated back home, or even talked to. Her fascination with him stemmed from the young girl-older man thing that she had seen in an old Ronald Coleman, Jean Arthur and Cary Grant movie. Ronald Coleman liked Jean and she liked him, but not in the same way- and especially with Cary Grant in the picture. Lenny was an older man, about 35, who could probably be a great teacher, but she was not willing to be his pupil. Kathleen remained very "proper" with Lenny, and did not plan to change.

167

Kathleen was beginning to find herself, even at this young age. She wanted more out of a relationship than just sex, and she was not going to settle for less. Kathleen wrote everything in that old ledger/diary. She wanted to be liked, but respected, and she understood that men didn't walk into a room with a woman's brains on his arm. Bottom line, Kathleen wanted to be more than window-dressing. This Kathleen wanted to finish school and be somebody that she could be proud of; not like her friend Dorothy. Of course going back to Ernest may be one way to start. The umpire was still confused despite the half-hearted proposal from Ernest.

Mrs. Fasse began her lesson on Yom Kippur and told stories of her family's flight from Russia to America. Apparently she had come from real aristocracy, but her husband's family was skilled laborers, cobblers of sorts, in shoemaking. "I guess you might say with the shoes, I really married beneath myself," she said, attempting to tell a joke as they went into the kitchen to prepare a dish. Kathleen got a word in edgewise, nervously, and asked Mrs. Fasse what she would do if the only man that she had had sexual relations with wanted her to marry him? Mrs. Fasse wiped her hands from having mixed up some ground chuck, and poured them both two tall glasses of lemonade. After first declaring that she did not want her to go back to Memphis, she then added that true love makes us do what our brain tells us we shouldn't. "If you truly love this man, and he has proven himself worthy of your love, then by all means-make preparations to go. But if not, then forget him. Your Ernest sounds like my Jacob- Jacob Levinsky- a man who tricked me into dropping my underwear and giving him my family jewels- literally and figuratively." Kathleen reacted, "You, Mrs. Fasse? There was someone else before Mr. Fasse?" She shushed Kathleen and walked to the front door to make certain that no one was coming in. "Come and sit at the dining room table with me; it's alright to bring the lemonade. Just get a coaster." The living and dining room were adjoined. The furniture was ivory and she rarely ate in the area accept on special occasions. Kathleen knew that she was special for Mrs. Fasse to let her drink in this room. From the way Mrs. Fasse sat-comfortably taking off her shoes, Kathleen sensed a long conversation was underway.

"I never talk about this, Minnie, because it's not something one would want to get out. The only other persons I've told what I'm about to tell you is my daughter, because I knew that she was about to give herself to this low-life of a boy- thank God she didn't- and of course my sister Minnie. At eighteen, most of the Jewish girls I knew were already engaged or promised to someone through a hired arranger- like a marriage broker. When my family came to America, I was not born yet. Mother was about three months with me and Minnie was eight years old. Mother had to sell quite a bit of the family jewels to help Daddy get here and set up, and that was okay, but after I was born, my mother wanted to make certain that my future would be more secure. She then, in a sense, sold me to the highest bidder —she thought making a pact with a broker would give me that security. After all, a broker would know the best Yiddish families- where all the wealth was. By the time I was thirteen, all I knew was that I was going to be a Levinsky. The Levinsky's real name was longer than that, but after arriving in America, most everyone's name was shortened.

We spent lots of time together, Jacob and I did- laughing and playing as teenagers do. But by the time I was seventeen,

Jacob had a reputation as a womanizer. He was three years older than I- more experienced and spoiled. I tell you that boy got everything he wanted and I was about to be his next possession. It was the evening of his brother Hershel's Bar Mitzpha. We were sitting in his father's car, making out, while the grownups were inside getting sloshed from Schnapps. My, oh my," she reminisced. "I mean, if Jacob kissed you-you were kissed. He kissed me until my knees knocked and my body trembled." Minnie injected, "You, Mrs. Fasse?" She replied, "Yes, me. I was about as ready as a match stuck into a hot stove, but I didn't let him. See everyone- my family, friends, the neighbors trusted us- I mean me- because they thought we were like brother and sister- no romance- but friends who would make a good couple one day. That was so far from the truth. He wanted me, and I wanted him. Jacob was tall, good looking and every other girl in the neighborhood wanted him. Well, anyway, we went to the roof, where we had birds and other pets and flowers that we tended. And there on top of the roof, before God, the sky and the birds, I got lost in his kisses, and I gave myself to him. It happened so fast that I couldn't tell you if there was anything good about it-then- but with what I know today- it was lousy! Lousy I tell you. I knew instantly that I had made the worst mistake of my life. The bastard snatched my panties up and ran away. At first, I didn't understand, but some time later I discovered that I was the only holdout in the neighborhood except for a girl named Esther- and she was homely as sin and pidgeon-toed, but she was nice, though. Jacob gave me the panties back about 2 weeks later, after I had given him a broach that belonged to my late grandmother- see, he blackmailed me. Ma and Papa were heartbroken. They thought that someone had stolen it- they never knew about what I did. I tried all I could to make Jacob give the broach back, but to no avail. Not long afterwards, I heard that he and Esther, whose father was an attorney, got married, supposedly because Jacob got her in trouble. Apparently she wasn't as homely as we thought." Minnie asked, "How…how did you and Mr. Fasse get together?" "That's a long story, but I can tell you this, he knew all about Jacob and the roof, but he wanted to marry me anyway, so I did, and –she said slowly- I don't regret it for one moment." Mrs. Fasse walked to her dresser and pulled out a cloth. She walked back to Kathleen and said, "What I learned was that a woman can be with a man who loves and respects her, and passion may come. I also learned that Mr. Fasse had tremendous power to retrieve things that I couldn't. Look." Inside the cloth was a broach with beautifully colored sets of pearls and diamonds. He gave me this on our first wedding anniversary. He never told me how he got it. I just knew that when I looked in his eyes that day, I knew that he loved me, that's all. That's what you should look for in a man, Minnie, or shall I say **Kathleen?**" If the expression '*my heart was in my throat*' could ever be literal, Kathleen became both the witness and victim simultaneously. Tears had welled up in both their eyes from the love story, but now, Kathleen said nothing. She just turned and ran to her room as quickly as her legs could take her and locked her door. She took her suitcase from the closet, tossed in some clothes, but there was little room for them. Kathleen had accumulated a lot more clothes than would fit her suitcase. She needed another one, but could not bring herself to open the door that Mrs. Fasse was now knocking on. Kathleen said nothing, but sat on the sofa with her head in hand. She knew that only Teddy really knew who she really was, and that he must have told his mother. Kathleen sat in utter disbelief of how she trusted him, and every word that her Grandmother had told her about trusting white people came back to haunt her. How could he tell, she thought, after all promises they made to keep some things secret? They had become close; as close as blood relatives- yet he betrayed her.

Kathleen could hardly see through her ears as Mrs. Fasse continued to knock on the door. "Honey, please, let me in, I am not angry with you. I've known for some time now. Please, open the door. I do have a key, you know, but I'd rather you let me in." Resolved that there was nothing else to hide anymore; Kathleen opened the door. She would later write about this night of confusion as a sense of relief and fear happening at simultaneously. Mrs. Fasse immediately put her arms around Kathleen, who could not stop crying. "Sit down here, dear." Mrs. Fasse shut the door and moved a chair close to Kathleen and held her hand.

Mrs. Fasse began, "To most of my people, I was known as the Gracie Allen –you know who she is, don't you? Kathleen nodded. "I was cute, fun- but not too bright upstairs- if you know what I mean. Well, some of that may be true, but I knew that I was awfully bright- and so was Gracie too. You can't be that funny and have that kind of timing and not be. The stupid can't play funny or dumb like Gracie, but the smart can. Gracie married George Burns, didn't she? From the moment I saw you at the agency, I could see a little girl who was hurting and running away from something. I watched how you would bite your fingernails on those nice hands and how your face wore every emotion that you felt- when you're

172

happy or when you're sad. Since you've been with us, I have grown to love you like a daughter. And I cannot say enough about how our Teddy loves you. He would protect you with his life, he would. And he would protect himself. Teddy has answered calls from your Ernest before, and he told him in no uncertain terms that you were otherwise engaged; that there was someone else in your life and to leave you alone." Kathleen began to speak, but Mrs. Fasse shushed her and whispered, since Teddy's room was next to Kathleen's. "Let me finish, dear. Now, I knew nothing about this until one day when you and Teddy went walking and this gentleman called. He and I had an interesting chat. Throughout the conversation, this Ernest had a slip of the tongue and called you Kathleen. I said nothing. I wanted to think that you might have told me one day-soon, when you felt safe enough; that you could trust me. Part of me wondered if you were in trouble with the law, so I...and forgive me... I launched an investigation- hoping not to find out anything. I suppose that I have watched enough James Bond and Alfred Hitchcock movies to know how to eliminate suspicion. But there was Teddy to think of, and I had to. Please, forgive me, child, but I had you checked out by some law enforcement friends of mine. I...I'm really ashamed about it, now, but I believed at the time that it was the best thing to do... to ease my mind. I had to protect Teddy." Kathleen was stunned and spoke abruptly. "Mrs. Fasse, if you knew all of this, why did you keep me here? Why did you investigate me if you thought that I was a...a criminal or that I might hurt Teddy or even Mr. Fasse? Why didn't you just fire me? How long ago did you ...investigate me?" Mrs. Fasse answered, "That doesn't really matter, dear just know that I trust you implicitly...

we all do, but Teddy always has. That boy loves you with his whole heart, and doesn't want to see anyone hurt you. Believe me, he wants you to be happy, just as Mr. Fasse and I do. Now, when you feel like it, you can tell me the whole story of why you changed your name and why you are using someone else's social security number. I think that you owe me that. Now about this Ernest..." Kathleen interrupted Mrs. Fasse-"No, Mrs. Fasse, I don't really feel like talking about Ernest right now, if you don't mind. Maybe tomorrow I can talk.

I would like to spend the night with Dorothy tonight-Ma'am-and I'd like to take the bus. I know that my day off is tomorrow, but I...I really need today off, Mrs. Fasse, if you don't mind-please?" Ms. Fasse hugged Kathleen again and agreed, but insisted on paying cab fare for her. That would amount to about twenty-five dollars or more, but she wanted to do it. Kathleen let her. "Oh, and Teddy didn't tell me anything, I told him yesterday, and he begged me not to tell you. He was afraid that you would leave- I hope he's not right-dear, for his sake, and ours. Oh, if Lenny calls, do you want me to give him the number over there?" Kathleen quickly replied, "No, no ma'am- well, yes, I guess, if you want."

The cab pulled in front of Dorothy's and the driver smiled as Kathleen handed him twenty- dollars and another five-dollar tip for carrying her bag. Dorothy met her at the door, immediately led Kathleen upstairs to her room, and told her to rest until lunch. Dorothy was not off work, so she had several chores to finish, which included preparing lunch. After Kathleen called Dorothy from the Fasse's, she, like Kathleen, asked for the rest of the afternoon off and her employers complied. Dorothy had all but wrapped this couple around her finger- so much so that she did not have to wear a uniform if she didn't want to and made as many long distance calls as her heart desired. In fact, the last few times Kathleen had visited her, she noticed that Dorothy seemed more like the lady of the manner- just doing whatever she wanted. She was wearing expensive clothes; clothes that she would never be able to afford, but Kathleen had so much on her mind, that she didn't bother to pursue Dorothy's obvious relationship development.

It was one o'clock before Dorothy woke Kathleen up. "Girl, come on down and eat- I have some fruit and chicken salad already ready." Kathleen commented on not being very hungry, but as often she and Dorothy had done- they sat at the table nibbled and talked about their love lives. Only this time Kathleen was concerned about her relationship with the Fasse family. "If you ask me," said Dorothy, "I think they have too damn much control over your life. They got you seeing Lenny, and intercepting your phone calls. Looks to me like another dose of Memphis- in a New York bottle. You think that white folk are different, but honey, this ought to prove it. Look how long this woman knew your real name and didn't open her mouth! Look how she was bent on getting you fixed up with that Black Jew to keep you from going home. It's all about control- I tell you. She knows that if you go, she won't have nobody to take care of Teddy- at least nobody that she trusts. It takes a lot to break in a new maid- I know- I mean housekeeper. These folk don't want to lose a good thing just like the white folk back home. You just wait- tell her that you want to go back to school and get your education- see what she says. I bet you she will show you the place where you can do it later. Don't tell me I don't know my white folk, girl. I major in white folk and minor in men. That's why I don't let these here get away with nothing. They ain't gon' make a fool out of me. I get what I need out of them, and I give them some of what they want from me- just enough to keep them in check. You' let your people know how sensitive you are, and how good you can be. That's why they feel that they should be all in your business. You shouldn't 'a never got so close with Ted, girl, never." Even though she thought that Shug was always giving her scatterbrained advice, Kathleen knew that some of what she said was true. She had become "comfortable" with the Fasse family-especially Teddy. But she could not help being the person that she was. Kathleen had not been raised to be a phony; that's why it was hard to accept being called a Supreme- to pretend for Lenny, or pretend to be coquettish with the badmouthing ladies at the dance for no reason. "I hate being a liar, Shug; and you know that. For Ms. Fasse to find who I really am makes me untrustworthy in her eyes and Teddy's. She'll probably tell her sister, her friends and other family members. I couldn't stand to stay there with all that. I think it's time to go back home." To Shug, *back* and *home* were two dirty words to be left unspoken. *Back home* meant poverty, a wounded relationship with a married man, and possibly getting her ass re-kicked by his wife, moving in with her Grandma Clemmie and all those grandchildren, or going back to her mother and eleven siblings in the two-bedroom home. To stay at either place meant sharing a bed with siblings or cousins who dipped stuff and pissed the bed on a continuing basis- not to mention the smelly farts from eating meatless meals of cornbread and beans six days a week. There was nothing about "back home" that Dorothy wanted or thought that Kathleen needed. It was Shug's convincing time and she was about to spend it well. "Do you want to call

Sonny and see if he is willing to get married before you leave for home? I really don't think that you' in love with the man anymore, if you ever was. It's like this, if you never taste but one fruit in your life how will you know that there are others that may be sweeter than the one you had? That's your problem right there, girl. You have the opportunity to just smell other fruit- not taste it-just smell it-that's all- and you won't do that. You' scared; I know what it's like to be scared too. If that man wants you, let him come after you. I ain't payin' a damn dime for a Negro (knee-gro) to come and get me. If he wants me, he better haul his ass up here on a white horse, a plane or a damn balloon or some'in'. That's what a mane would do if he really wanted you. And as far as Mrs. Fasse ass goes, I think the woman was trying to tell you that she already forgave you. If she didn't, she would have tried to kick your ass out before now. Instead, with they' controlling ass, tried to hook you up with Lenny. Let me tell you something girl, I didn't want to say nothing, but that man is too pretty for words. He is got more than titties on his mind, believe me. The man is 'strange as a $3- bill; a switch-hitter, and I ain't talking about baseball. I peeped that at the introduction. Lenny called here, you know, just before you came." Kathleen became defensive, "How do you know he's a …? Everybody is not strange, 'cause you say so." Dorothy did not let up. "Look, the man asked if he could come over, after he called your house, and Mrs. Fasse told him you were here. I told him that you would call him back. I sort of had a conversation with him. 'Man got enough freaky shit in him to start a freak factory, I tell ya'." Kathleen countered her statement with, "But didn't you tell me once that everybody's got a little freak in them?" Kathleen reacted with, "That's terrible, Shug. You just saw him one time; that's all, and you say something like that." Dorothy quickly replied, "'Don't take but one time to see somebody before they' true colors come out, and believe me, that man's colors are very bright; like the sun. Tell you what, 'just suggest something freaky with him when he gets here, he'll jump on it like a spider on a fly. Watch what I tell you. Kathleen was not only disappointed, but angry with her for even suggesting such a thing. "Look, when he comes, just play along with whatever I say, and watch. Okay? Then if I'm lying I will apologize to you and him both." Kathleen nodded, but wanted to talk about her situation with Mrs. Fasse. Kathleen waited and wondered, could she be deceived again about a man's character?

The doorbell rang after 6:00pm, and Lenny walked in dressed immaculately, but he was not alone. A very good looking white man who reminded Kathleen of the actor John Garfield came in and introduced himself as Joey. He was wearing a brown leather vest, a cap, and tight, tight brown slacks that bulged on the left from either a long pistol or a member that needed larger size slacks. In contrast, Lenny wore a traditional white shirt, suit and tie, with shoes that shined like new money. Kathleen found herself looking at Lenny more closely than ever- since Dorothy's declaration, but soon dismissed it with the macho-man persona of Joey. Obviously Italian, he was handsome, did not smile a lot, but had piercing light brown eyes and lots of hair. Lenny introduced him, as Dorothy took his coat and cap. Lenny put his arm around Kathleen's waist and Dorothy ushered everyone into the den. Kathleen thought about her first time going out with Lenny, his display of affection on the beach, and the compliments he gave her. At no time during the course of that evening could she recollect clues of what Dorothy was talking about. He appeared to only to be interested in her, but then, there had never been any male company around to compare his actions except Teddy or Mr. Fasse. Kathleen wanted to call Teddy and ask what he thought, but the awkward situation at the Fasse's home kept her from dialing the number. Kathleen knew that no matter what the situation was with Lenny, she had bigger fish to fry. Her relationship with Mrs. Fasse was all consuming. Dorothy had managed to divert her attention with the curiosity of Lenny's sexuality, and Kathleen would have to deal with the male guests for the evening.

Lenny never turned Kathleen loose until they all went into what Lenny called "the playroom." Sitting on the semi-circular sofa, Dorothy offered to make drinks to which both Lenny and Joey replied, "Make mine Scotch" and pinched each other. Lenny continued, "It's been one of those days; a good stiff drink about now would ease the tension." Kathleen looked at Dorothy, wondering what tension that he was talking about. She was disappointed in herself for taking part in this unplanned investigation into Lenny's sexuality. Throughout the evening, Kathleen hung on to every word Lenny and Joey spoke and analyzed every move they made. She thought about all of the stereotypical rantings she had heard from her great uncles and brothers about "sissies" after seeing two effeminate men in her neighborhood-"Peaches and Pumpkin" they were called. In the neighborhood, these men lived a peaceful existence; no one harassed them, but always seemed to chuckle or shake their head when passing their house. Homo-sexuals may have existed in Kathleen's neighborhood, but she had yet to encounter a "switchhitter" as Shug had eluded.

About an hour and a half had passed along with several drinks since their arrival. They were watching television when Lenny suddenly wanted to dance. Dorothy stated several times that her "people" would not be back until the afternoon of the next day, and the house was at their disposal. Turning off the television, Dorothy played one of Stevie Wonder's slow tunes, to which Lenny extended his arm for her to dance with him. Kathleen watched as he held Dorothy tighter. Was Lenny trying to make her jealous by dancing the way he was with Dorothy? Kathleen made no overture of jealousy, but Lenny kept staring at her. Joey stood and extended his arm to Kathleen and began slow-dancing, holding her very close. Each time Dorothy turned toward Kathleen, she would wink and point to how Lenny was acting. The more liquor he drank, the more graphic his conversation became. He commented on Dorothy's protruding derriere and complimented her on her choice of perfume; occasionally sniffing her like a dog in heat. Suddenly, Lenny stretched out his arm for Kathleen, but Joey did not turn her loose. Somehow, the four of them gradually became locked in an embrace with Lenny beginning a kind of "kiss around" on the cheek: Lenny to Dorothy- Dorothy to Joey- Joey to Kathleen, who shook her head no. Lenny continued to try and persuade her. He jokingly grabbed Joey and kissed him on the cheek and said, "See, he won't bite unless you want him to." Out of curiosity, Kathleen kissed Joey's cheek and he spoke, "Now, doesn't this make one great picture, two fine women and two fine men."

Someone dimmed the lights, as Lenny staggered on to the sofa and said, "Let's switch partners." He crawled over Joey to Kathleen and put his arms around her waist. If you just say the word, I can make you feel good right here and now." He kissed her on the lips; Kathleen hated the smell of the liquor on his breath. She wanted to be polite, but pushed him away gently. Suddenly Joey who was already kissing Dorothy turned to Lenny and said, "Time to switch again." The two men began kissing each other, tongue and all. The quiet in the room was as loud as a gunshot. Lenny then turned to Kathleen and tried to unbutton her blouse while biting on her neck. Kathleen immediately rose and said, "I don't know what the hell your problem is, but I ain't your solution." She left the room, and while running upstairs she heard Dorothy tell them to leave.

Ten minutes or so later, Dorothy entered her room almost chanting, "I told you so, I told you so." Kathleen said nothing; she just sighed and turned her head away. Dorothy was quiet for a moment, too then she asked Kathleen a question: "You liked Lenny, didn't you? Kathleen was silent. "I know. It's always disappointing to find out somebody is a go'damn freak. It wouldn't have been so bad, except he comes across like so much man. Kathleen was still quiet, but as soon as Dorothy brushed her teeth and got into the other twin bed, Kathleen turned over and began talking. "Do you have some kind of radar that picks up on freaky people? How could they do that?" Dorothy answered, "They' swingers, girl, that's how," Dorothy replied. "I have been here before, girl, and believe me, what I learned from that time they write in dirty books. That's how I can spot them." Kathleen asked, "What makes people pretend to like you, or love you or even care about you when all they really care about is what THEY want and what THEY want to do? What's wrong with me? Do I have a big sign that draws guys who like freaky stuff? I admit that I thought Lenny was freaky, but a switch-hitter? What is wrong with me that I can't see anything until I'm in the middle of it? I don't want a freak. Yes, I liked the guy, because he's my boss' friend, and he's good-looking, and he ...he was flattering to me. I just wanted to have a good time with him; have fun." Dorothy added, "And so did he and so did his boy, Joey," Dorothy added. Kathleen began to explain, "Shug, at first, he treated me like a lady, he did. And I really needed someone to do that. I wasn't planning on marrying the guy or even seeing him for a long period. You know... ever since my Mama died, my life has been like a game of bad pitchers; bad hitters, fouls; just one bad move after another. I started lying, making stupid decisions, worrying about what people thought about me, and I feel like my Mama is at me saying, "My little girl is a whore or not fit to be with a decent man." Kathleen's eyes filled with tears. "Then I think about my Grandmother; I miss her so, so, much, but she would rather think that I liked women than think good about me. The men I meet expect me to go to bed with them, because I look like I know all about sex. I'm so unhappy inside most of the time, because I had to grow up and be grown when I was a few days from being 18 when Mama died. I'm sick of it all! I'm so sick of pretending. I want not to worry about anything; I want somebody to love me, just love me for me. I want to have something someday just like the people my Grandmother work for, or like Mrs. Fasse or even these crazy people you work for – like this mansion. And if I get all of that, I still want my Mama! But I know that that will never happen. Being crooked and scheming and lying is not who I am, who I have become! Grandma used to say that you can spend money, and you can always get more, but if you spend your time wrong- wrong is what you get back. I thought that coming here to New York would erase everything wrong from back home. But it looks like no matter where I go; where I live, things can still go wrong. Shug, I…I just want to go back home." The room was silent.

Dorothy stared at her and prepared herself for bed, crawling slowly under the covers. Kathleen spoke again, not looking at Dorothy. "I'm going to straighten things out with my Grandmother and Ms. Fasse." Shug quickly asked, "What about Ernest?" Kathleen replied just as promptly, "What about him? I' got loose ends to tie up here, girl. I need to change me. I don't have any one to really tell me about what my body could or should feel as a woman. It's kind of embarrassing, you know what I mean?" Shug added, "I know. I try to help you, girl, but my take on men may be a little different from yours. I might get some and not see anybody afterwards. Sex is sex, but see, what YOU want to do is to make love. The difference is that sex is just raw shit, but love is…love is emotional. Didn't know that I knew those words, did ya'? 'Live in the house with a freaky doctor, like I do, and everything gets explained. Some of this shit you gon' have to just pick up as you go. Don't sweat it girl, the average Joe and Jill like sex. So don't be upset 'cause you feel what comes natural. I'm sleepy. Let's talk in the morning." Kathleen closed her eyes, but going home was on her mind, and was not about to leave.

Kathleen woke early, gathered her things and bid Shug a good day. As she waited for the bus to come, a sick feeling arose in the pit of her stomach. Aside from the fact that she hadn't eaten any breakfast, the thought of facing Mrs. Fasse was getting to her. Kathleen had grown to really respect her employer as a friend, a mother figure, and someone she could learn from. Cultural, artistic, religious and other social subjects just poured from Mrs. Fasse's mouth each day. Kathleen soaked everything up like a new sponge. The last thing that Kathleen wanted was for Mrs. Fasse to have a bad opinion of her. One thing for certain, she had decided to come clean, about her name, and about their friend Lenny. She wanted her to know that just because Lenny was their friend, he was not necessarily the man she or Mr. Fasse thought that he was. Kathleen wanted to free her soul of any deceit. Kathleen was going to write that night; about hypocrites and how anyone could be one, depending on the circumstances. Kathleen also knew that she had to do something else, she had to hurry back to Memphis- if for nothing more than to see her Grandmother.

CHAPTER VII

Sliding Into Home

Before Kathleen was to leave, Dorothy asked her a big favor. The Shaeffer's were having a party in two weeks and wanted some help. Kathleen started to decline, but she remembered having asked to work the next time there was a party. She had planned on leaving soon, but she had not made all of her plans known to Mrs. Fasse or Teddy. The Fasse's were leaving town for a couple of days, so they suggested that Kathleen go to Dorothy's. They feared that she would leave them, so whatever Kathleen asked, they were willing to grant. Kathleen agreed to go to Dorothy's, then called her, but could not reach her. She told Mrs. Fasse that if she could not get Dorothy, she would stay home and go the next day. The Fasse's decided that all conversation about Kathleen's pseudonym would be tabled until their return. Kathleen was making up her mind whether to go home to get married or to forget Ernest and stay in New York. Kathleen's strong desire for an education, to become sophisticated, to travel, or to marry a man who really loved her, left her somewhat confused. Going to Dorothy's seemed like the next base to cover for advice. She was Kathleen's only real connection to home, and she really needed that now.

Dorothy's line was busy when Kathleen made the next call; there was another phone number- a private number that Shug had told her about, but she had never tried calling it before, and could not find it. Kathleen decided to go on before dark and the buses would stop running. There was loud music heard outside, when she arrived at the front door of the mansion. After ringing the doorbell, she noticed that no one came to the door, but she wondered if the bell would be heard with the music playing so loudly. Dorothy had a habit of playing loud music on several other occasions. She had mentioned to Kathleen that if she ever had trouble getting in, so she used it. She put her overnight case in the hall as she entered the mansion, and followed the trail of the loud music, which came from the den. An overpowering aroma of honey and herbs filled the air. As Kathleen came closer to the den, she could hear familiarly faint voices. The door to the Den was slightly open and the room was smoky and dark except for the lighted candles on the table. There on the sofa and floor lay bodies, sweating, laughing, moaning, groaning, in positions only seen in the two dirty books Kathleen sneaked a peak at in one of her grandmother's employer's son's room. Kathleen had never really seen pornographic movies she only heard about them, but it appeared that she had suddenly stepped right into one when she reached the dimly lit Den door. To her right were three people wrapped in an embrace so complicated that only a contortionist would be able to understand. One black woman was being serviced by the mouth of a large white male as her mammary glands were stroked by a white female- simultaneously. After some careful examination, Kathleen put her hand over her mouth and frowned with shock after noticing that the two people were Dorothy's employers, Mr. and Mrs. Shaeffer, and the woman on the floor was Dorothy! To Kathleen's left were two men fawning over each other on the floor along with a very slim blonde woman in some trio act that did not involve singing. Kathleen wanted to scream, but wouldn't. She tightened her hand on her mouth and just walked right out without anyone hearing her gasp or her footsteps. She wanted to run, but the fear of noise made her tiptoe through the hall. She wanted to get out of the house as quickly as possible, but there were no more buses funning. She would have to call a cab or the Fasses to get her. Leaning up against the wall, she was startled by the barking of the dog. She managed to settle him down, when suddenly a hand touched her shoulder and she screamed. It was Lenny with a woman whom he pointed to go back into the direction of the den. "What's wrong; you look like you've seen a ghost? She didn't say that you were going to be here." He looked at the suitcase as Kathleen picked it up hurriedly. Kathleen looked around and there stood all of the den members, some half-naked and others parading their birthday suits as if they were used to seeing each other in this stage of undress. Kathleen focused on the floor, trying not to look at them, and she began apologizing for arriving unannounced. "I...I'm truly sorry. I didn't know...I'll just call a cab...and... uh..." Dorothy entered holding a towel around her, and interrupted, "Would you all leave us alone, please. Go, please. Katy...I mean... I'll be with you in a minute..." There was a slight pause, then Kathleen took her suitcase and purse to the room. She could hear Shug run to the restroom and run water for a long time. She sat, feeling sick to her stomach, more uncomfortable than she had ever been in her life. She wanted to cry or yell, but to whom and about what? Lenny was still there, and reached for her hand; but Kathleen would not hold it. "I'm sorry, baby. I know that this may not be your cup of tea." Kathleen cringed and shook her head as if the sights from the Den could somehow leave her. Lenny continued, "I won't defend anyone 'cause I'm sure that you wouldn't listen anyway. This is New York, baby- a melting pot for all types of sexual appetites, and people from all over the world. Unless you want to be a part of the pot, stay away from it. Your friend, Dorothy- well, this is her second trip to the Big Apple, and she likes how it smells, how it tastes- and you don't. I think that's sweet and charming, but not what we died in the wool swingers want. I'm sorry to disappoint you, but what people do in the privacy of their home is just that- private. Believe me, a part of would like to be like you- gung-ho on monogamy, but it's just a small part. I'm really sorry that you had to…" Suddenly Dorothy entered in a robe. Lenny tried to kiss Kathleen's hand, but she pulled away, and he left for the Den. "I… I've got to go, but the buses have stopped running," Kathleen slowly uttered. Shug stared at Kathleen, both of them tearing up. "I'll get you a cab, I've got the money. I suppose you don't want Lenny to take-'course not." Kathleen tried to leave anyway, but Shug stopped her. "Please, wait, please, Katy." Kathleen pulled away from her. She really could not look at Shug, so she picked up her overnight bag, when Shug yelled. "I'm not like you, Katy, I'm not! I'm sorry, I really am. I would never have wanted you to know about this, never." Kathleen interrupted, "Why, Shug? Why?" Kathleen asked with her back turned to Shug. " I don't really know. It's about money, and just doing something.

When I was here before, I met some people, and they turned me on to swinging. I kind of got fed up with it, and came back to Memphis. Then I met the love of my life, and I was willing to be shared, ethough because he just happened to have a wife, and well you know the rest. When I came back here, I didn't know that they the Shaeffer's were swingers, but believe me, we all kind of sense these things after a while. So, I... that's how I knew about Lenny. He knew the Shaeffer's." Kathleen turned and looked at Shug and asked again, but why... why women?" Shug replied with a straight face, "I have dabbled in that world, Kathleen, with most girls that I got tight with- most- except you. You are... you were like my sister. I didn't feel that with you." Kathleen rushed to the front door and onto the walkway, as Shug yelled her name to stop and listen. Kathleen threw down the bag and interrupted Shug, who was begging her not to walk in the dark. Kathleen pointed her finger in Shug's face and said, "That's why my uncle said what he did, and Ernest, and my grandmother- they all knew about you! I was too damn dumb to know. You should have trusted me enough to tell me, Shug. Did you think that I would stop being your friend? I ain't never liked the fact that you were going with a married man, or had a reputation for being easy, but you were MY friend. I shared my thoughts with you, we slept in the same bed and you couldn't tell me? It makes me feel like everybody was laughing behind my back, "Dumb little Katy, her friend messes with women, and she doesn't even know it- everybody knew it but ME!" Shug quickly remarked, "That's the difference between you and me, Katy. You give a damn what people think, and I don't! But I do care what you think, I really do. Tell me, Katy, would you really have stayed friends with me if I had told you?

189

You ' smart, square, and dreaming 'bout goals and what you can be. You said you made As and Bs in school, well, hell, I barely went to school, barely ate. The only thing I was good at was fucking, and my grandmother's brother made damn sho' that I was good at it by the time I was 13. From 10 to 13 exactly- 'till his old ass finally up and died- and good riddance! A child can get mixed feelings about sex, you know; about what feels good to you, but it's not good for you. I used to ask myself how something like this that feels so good be bad for me? Then you get pregnant and it dies before it can start to grow inside you. Then the doctor tells you that you can't never have a child because all of your shit, your birthing parts are so damaged that you can't even carry a baby. See, Katy, I ain't you. I ain't you! I didn't tell you because I was scared…yeah, me. Scared of losing a real friend who needed me to be her ears in a place she couldn't hear, eyes for what she didn't see, and a heart for understanding. Be a real sister- when my real ones had been told that I-they' big sister was a 'ho' and they better not grow up to be like me. You never really knowed why I didn't stay with my Mama and Daddy, did ya'? You were so lucky to done had a Mama who loved you-even dead in her grave, I bet she loves you still. Mine's living, but she won't even talk to me. She believed that I enticed my uncle to do what he did to me." Kathleen quickly added, "But you-you have a choice, Dorothy. You can either let that uncle control your life, what happened to you, or you can run if you want. Run… run toward something good or away from everything you know that means you no good. I ain't gonna judge you, Shug. I have been running every since the night they told me that my Mama died, and I'm tired of running, 'cause no matter where I go, I ain't got no home! I'm still your friend,

Shug, but I just could never be a part of this, never." Just then, a cleaned up dressed Lenny appeared from nowhere and offered to take Kathleen home. "Look, I know you don't want to ride with me, but I promise that I won't bother you. Cab drivers aren't even safe to ride with at this hour." Kathleen reluctantly took the offer, but as Lenny walked toward the car, she looked at Dorothy's tear stained face, and Dorothy shook her head for Katy to take Lenny's offer. Kathleen told him okay, and somehow she knew that this would be her last trip to the mansion- maybe even the last time she would see Dorothy before going home. The two girls looked at each other as Lenny pulled the car around. They did not wave, just looked, as Shug turned around and walked quickly into the mansion.

When they arrived at the apartment, few words had been spoken, but Lenny was determined to be the gentlemen and see Kathleen to the door. "I'm sorry, Memphis, I apologize for all of New York. Go home- this is not a place for good girls like you. I wish that I was a good boy- I really do." Kathleen asked, "Can I ask you something, Lenny?" Lenny nodded. "Why did you make me think that you were....that you didn't like Teddy and stuff, when you ... you obviously swing with people who are not just black. Why did you?" Lenny answered, "I wanted to know if you were really that little Memphis girl that I thought you were and how you felt about that boy-Teddy. I wanted to know if you might be ripe for swinging or what. Who knows what would have happened. I liked you, Kathleen, from the time I met you, and I wanted you to like me, for the Fasse's sake if nothing else. That's all." Lenny hugged her, turned around and added, "but there are really people who think that they can say anything to you and get away with it. I don't like upstarts- no matter what color they are. So don't think that it was just the white boy I was lambasting. It could have been anybody."

Kathleen thanked Lenny, used her key to let herself in, walked straight to her room and closed her eyes to flashes from the past months darting through her head, interrupting her sleep. She began to write in her ledger/diary about the past few days while it was fresh in her mind. Mrs. Fasse noticed that she came back, and asked Kathleen if there was something wrong. Kathleen answered that she would tell her about it later and that she just wanted to come back home. She didn't have the heart to tell Mrs. Fasse about the incident at Dorothy's right then or anything about the evening. When Mrs. Fasse left, Kathleen noticed that the red light was lit up on the phone, which indicated that someone had called. She thought of the calls that she wanted to make-to Ernest, to her grandmother, Mrs. Clemmie, and the terminal about the bus schedule for Memphis. Kathleen thought of slipping away, not telling her employers anything, but she knew that the Fasse's had been too good to her. She needed to say goodbye to them- especially to Teddy.

"I'm coming home Mrs. Clemmie; my Grandmother said she wants me to move back home with her... I don't know- What? I can't believe that he called you. All I know is I'm coming home to Memphis! I miss all of you, too. I have to go now; 'see you soon." Kathleen found the time that her bus would be leaving. Being in the house alone gave Kathleen time to think about what to do- about her life. The Fasses left the next morning after the mansion incident, and were slated to return the next day. Kathleen planned to tell them everything after thoroughly cleaning the apartment.

She packed all of her things, except for what she would wear home.

Just as the evening's sunset, Kathleen put the dishes in the sink to wash. She was never quite comfortable with using the dishwasher for herself, choosing instead to wash the dishes she had just used for her dinner. She washed them slowly, hoping to stretch out the evening by keeping busy. She was determined not to call Dorothy or Lenny; choosing instead to watch television. A hot buttered batch of Jiffy Pop popcorn and a glass of soda were Kathleen's only company as she watched the World Series. It was baseball, the sport that reminded her of home, of legs that were too short for running after bunting a ball; and her legs that had to hit a home run not to be put out. And here Kathleen was- running again, but running back home. If Teddy were there with her, they'd be watching the Series with him yelling, swearing, and tossing pillows at the television, which he could not see. Already Kathleen had begun to regret the plan to leave; she knew that she would miss Teddy more than anyone else she had met.

Not even the ball game could hold her attention. Kathleen dozed off on the sofa thinking about last evening's revelations. Awakened by the doorbell, she looked through the peephole. She couldn't believe her eyes- there he was, in the flesh; as tall, black and sharply dressed as ever- Ernest! She ran into the bathroom to check her breath, switched her mouth with toothpaste and ran back to the peephole. When Kathleen opened the door, he lifted her up into his arms and held her tightly declaring his love for her. He asked her to marry him as soon as possible. Ernest apologized for everything that he had ever done to make her unhappy and chanted his sorrow for his foolish actions. He then helped her with her luggage, as Kathleen wrote Teddy a note and slid it under his door. He couldn't read it, but he surely would ask his parents to do so. Ernest whisked her off in a waiting cab and then on to the airport. Kathleen couldn't believe what was happening- but as he held her, she still wasn't certain that a life with Ernest was what she wanted.

Suddenly, Kathleen awoke to a humming television and the loud ring of her phone. After all, Kathleen had just experienced something very confusing- but realized that it was just what it was- a dream. There was no Ernest or any such proposal or ride to the airport. A familiar voice on the other end of the phone asked how she felt and when or if she was coming back to Memphis. She said that she would come back-soon, though she did not volunteer the exact time of her arrival. Kathleen told the party on the phone that she would call after she got home. She ended the conversation with, "Thanks for calling; I have to go, now, bye."

This time the doorbell rang and it was no dream, it was Dorothy. Kathleen reluctantly let her in. "What do you want, Shug?" Kathleen asked. Dorothy eyes were filled with tears as she stared at Kathleen. She asked Kathleen if she could sit down simultaneously. "I know that you didn't expect me to come, and I didn't expect to be here, but here I am," Dorothy announced. "Kathleen, I don't want to lose you as a friend, as a sister, but I am not going to apologize for doing what I do if it doesn't directly have anything to do with you. But you were right-and I'm just sorry that I didn't tell you about me. I know that you are kind of like a prude about sex, but..." Kathleen interrupted, "I never told you that I was a prude; I was just a virgin when we met, that's all. I can't help it if I haven't laid up with everything in pants. Although, for you

I guess pants and skirt would be about right. No wonder Ernest didn't want me 'round you. He knew all the time what you were a..." "What am I, Kathleen, huh? What am I? You don't know; you don't live inside of me! What makes a woman be with another woman is something I ain't gonna try to explain. Maybe it's because the first time I really ever felt like somebody cared about my feelings, it came from a woman. It's not something I'm all that damn proud of, but at least I'm not living a lie like you." Kathleen was so shocked at the insinuation that she was almost speechless, but managed to blurt, "I don't like women like that-that way, and I ain't never given you a reason to think that I do, have I?" Dorothy followed with a quick correction, "I don't mean that you like women, I mean that you act like you don't like sex, but every time you tell me about the men who have been in your life, the wet drawers you had from all that kissing and shit gave you the- what's that exact word? The 'tingles.' Well welcome to the world of sex, baby, because that what sex does-it makes you 'tingle,' act a damn fool, make loud sounds and it feels damn good! I don't care if it's from a man, a woman, or from your damn self. You know, you sit here and try to act like I'm so-oo bad, so wrong, well maybe I am, but that does not make you any better than me." Kathleen argued, "Never said that I was better than you! I never told you that! You had that old stupid notion. But I am not as bad as you-that's one thing. I don't sleep with everything and everybody and try to justify it. Unmarried sex is a sin, no matter who does it. And having sex with married men is- well you know it's not right either." Dorothy injected, "So having it with single men makes it right? That's the shit I'm talking about, Kathleen! That "I'm better than you' attitude" you got! I could stand for you to

195

correct me, I really could, if you was saying I was wrong morally or church wrong, not because you are so right. Do you understand; am I making myself clear?" Kathleen turned away from Dorothy and said nothing, but just as Dorothy headed for the door, Kathleen told her to wait. Kathleen was very angry, but deep down she knew what Dorothy meant. Kathleen had been judging Dorothy by comparing their vices and her standards. Kathleen knew that Dorothy was right, and if she really wanted to save their friendship, she was going to have to accept Dorothy as she was. "Whether I like what you do or not, Shug, I think that you...you're right about how I have been acting or what I think. And I'm sorry. I guess that I wanted to be a good girl until marriage so much, and I'm so damn mad at myself for doing what I said I would never do. I'm even more upset that I feel what I feel- at times. My great aunt always acts so self-righteous, and nobody in the family can stand her. I really don't have control over what I feel, but I want to control what I do; how I behave. Do I make sense?" Dorothy shook her head, and both girls stared at each other and hugged. They went back to the sofa, sat down with their hands folded together. "I'm sorry too if I hurt your feelings, Kathleen, I didn't..." Kathleen interrupted, "No, you were right. It was a shock, but I guess it shouldn't have anything to do with our friendship. I have a lot to work out; feelings I never had, what I want out of life. I really thought that coming up here to New York would give me that. That I wouldn't have to run away from anything anymore; that I could find love or it would find me... I'm really just kinda like a kid in a woman's body- all mixed up. I don't think that I really love Ernest. I think that I want to because he's the only man I have ever been with like that. He's not exactly the kind of man I want." Shug asked, "What kind do you want? Not Lenny, I hope?" Kathleen quickly answered, "No! No ma'am indeed not. I want an education, so I won't be this dumb black girl from the south wherever I go. I want...I want to be sophisticated, and not easy to take advantage of...not so trusting; not shocked at everything. I'm leaving sooner than I planned-tomorrow or the next day. And I want us to stay friends, Shug, no matter what. But, I don't have to accept, uh, lifestyles; what I don't like, Shug. There's nothing wrong with that, is there?" Shug answered, "No, girl, not at all." And who knows, maybe I'll find out some things about myself too. But you, girl, you will probably get what you want-just hold on, it will come. You gonna tell Mrs. Fasse about leaving when they get back tomorrow?" Kathleen shook her head no. "At first, I thought about telling her everything before, but I think that I'll call them from the station, tell them where I left a note for them. I'll leave Teddy a message on the tape recorder in his room. I swear I hate to leave that boy. He's so sweet, and... and I'm gonna break his heart, but I can't face him. I won't go anywhere if I see those beautiful eyes of his. They all 'been so good to me, but I want to see my family. My things are packed." Dorothy added, "I'll call Mama and ask her to send somebody to meet you at the- bus- Kathleen interrupted, " Someone will be at the station when I arrive." Dorothy paused and looked at Kathleen, "Oh, well, alright! I'm gon' miss you, but I understand. Memphis ain't gonna never be my speed, girl, and New York may not ever be yours, but let's keep in touch-okay?" Kathleen nodded her head, and they both wiped their eyes as Dorothy left.

When Shug left, Kathleen realized that growing people change and they lose touch. Kathleen knew that she would try to stay in contact with Dorothy even for a short while, but eventually that would change, too.

The next day, Kathleen went downstairs to help Mrs. Fasse bring some shopping bags upstairs. She had dropped Mr. Fasse at Waulbaums to pick up something he wanted from the Deli, so it was just her and Teddy in the car. While in the elevator, she told Mrs. Fasse that she was going back home, but she would give her two weeks' notice so that she could get someone else to replace her. Kathleen also asked her to tell Teddy that she was going for a visit, and that she would be coming back in about a month. Mrs. Fasse acted as if this was no surprise, but did not want to lie to Teddy. She did not want to tell him the truth either. Teddy was still downstairs with Michael, the doorman, who always helped with Teddy, but took time to talk with him about the latest Ham radio equipment, since they both shared the hobby or to get the mail. Mrs. Fasse looked at Kathleen, stared at each other, and looked away. They went back downstairs to get a few more things out of the trunk, but Mrs. Fasse suddenly took Teddy's hands and spoke to him, while Michael was there. "Kathleen and I have something to tell you when we get upstairs, honey. I'm going to pick up Daddy at Waulbaums, and we'll tell you together" "Mom, what is it? Kathleen was begging with her eyes not to tell Teddy, who kept on asking. "Micheal?" Mrs. Fasse asked, "Would you be so kind as to help take Teddy upstairs while I go and pick up Mr. Fasse from Waulbaum's. He was picking up a few things to celebrate the Series, you know. The Orioles won. Uh...I'll be right back." Teddy always lit up when Kathleen was with him. Micheal followed suit as Teddy urged his mother to hurry and get his Dad before he bought out the store.

When they got into the apartment, and after some badgering from Teddy, Kathleen said that she had to wait until his parents got there. When the door opened, Teddy said, "Now you can tell me what it is. They all sat down in the living room and Mrs. Fasse told Teddy that they were going to send Kathleen on a little trip; that she had been working so hard, and maybe a couple of weeks away from the house, she would not be so homesick. Teddy gave out a big, "No!" and went to his room and slammed the door. "I knew that it would break his heart." Kathleen asked Ms. Fasse to forgive her, but she explained why she could not have waited to tell Teddy that she was giving her notice. "Why now when he just got home? If you…if don't go right now, Mr. Fasse and I will fly you back home in two or three weeks. We don't want to look for anyone else right now. After all, didn't you tell me that Teddy kept your secret? Don't you think that you owe him a little more of your time, owe us- after all, we did not fire you after you lied to us. Sweetie, you once told me that you were always running from place to place, and you would explain later. Well, you don't have to run from here. You can walk and we all can take it, we can. We want you here for selfish reasons. For Teddy, to be like our daughter, to be the person we can care for, because our son is so much the better because of you. Teddy has become more self-sufficient, loyal and…and softer. It's been hell at times when he's thrown tantrums. Your being here has helped him with that; helped us. I understand you more than you know. Tell him please, or he'll lose faith and the old Teddy will come back, the weak one, who doesn't eat when he can't express himself or God forbid starts back on disposable diapers when he really withdraws. He can manage with us, but he won't if he thinks

199

that he ran you away. I'll give you anything I have if you'll go to him." "I want to go now, Mrs. Fasse," Kathleen insisted. If I wait any longer, it will just make it harder." She marched to his door, and knocked softly.

Teddy told her to come in and immediately asked. "Why are you leaving now? Kathleen was shocked and started to speak, only to be interrupted by Teddy. "I can put two and two together, you know. You were leaving without telling me, weren't you?" Kathleen answered, "Yes, but it was because I-" Teddy interrupted, "I knew it, because I could feel it, inside- I could. Well, if you want to go back home, I can understand, I'm 15 and I'm smart and I don't need an ugly black nursemaid around to baby me anymore-I'm not a baby, do you hear-me?" Teddy turned away from her, sitting on the side of the bed frozen and still. The room was silent for a few seconds; then Kathleen took a few steps toward him. "I love you, Teddy; you're the very best man friend I ever had. Teddy injected-"I'm just a boy." "You're more of a man than any one I have ever met-you're trustworthy, generous loyal and..." "Yeah, yeah, I'm a damn Boy Scout, a St. Bernard; put a damn leash on me, because that's what you just described," Teddy blurted out. "I'm so sorry if I hurt you," Kathleen said softly, "but I have to go, Teddy. I don't even know if I will make it back, but you've taught me so much that I take with me. How you defended me; kept my secrets. I love you, Teddy. Please, forgive me, but you are so smart, and I know that one day- soon, it was going to be almost impossible to leave you. I think just now, I know what I want. I want a Teddy in my life to treat me the way you have, and I won't, I promise, that I won't settle for less. I..." Kathleen touched him on the shoulder, but he jerked away. She walked toward his door and his parents were standing outside in the hallway. At that moment, one could have almost heard the tiniest of pin falling on the carpeting. Kathleen was almost blinded by the water that trickled down her face, as she leaned against the living room wall. Suddenly, Teddy walked in his stocking feet to the living room; then he called her name ever so softly. "Kathleen?" Kathleen turned, wiped her eyes and gazed at Teddy. He was not crying, but had his arms outstretched for her to come to him and she did, as fast as her legs could carry her. They stood there holding each other as his parents watched. Kathleen could feel him trembling, and she could also feel his member growing. He whispered in her ear after hearing his parents' return- "Walk me back to my room, I'm sorry. I didn't mean for this to happen." Kathleen did so. They shut the door, and he sat on one of his twin beds with a pillow to hide his predicament. "Call me, anytime, but don't write. I don't want Mom and Dad to know what we talked about. And if you do come back to Long Island, please, come and see me. Okay?" Kathleen told him okay, kissed him on both his cheeks, then on his lips and left his room.

Kathleen told the Fasse's that she could still take the bus; that a plane would cost too much. They wouldn't hear of it. Kathleen went to her room where she remained until Mrs. Fasse knocked with news about the flight. The takeoff would be early, and she would be taking Kathleen to the airport in the morning. "I think the sooner the better, dear. We all discussed this and decided that if we wait two weeks, it would make things worse for Teddy." She asked if she could help Kathleen pack, but she wouldn't let her. They finished and walked to the elevator with the bag and put it in the car. Obviously there were things that Mrs. Fasse wanted to say that she did not want Teddy to hear. They talked for about 10 minutes, came back upstairs and waited for the morning.

Sleep escaped her for much of the night, but Kathleen still arose, showered, and realized that the clothes she wanted to wear were in her bags. She looked at the ones that she had on and decided to change and asked Mrs. Fasse for the keys to get something else to wear. Mrs. Fasse was up already drinking her morning coffee and gave the key to Kathleen. She saw Micheal immediately after getting off the elevator buttoning his jacket preparing for work, and thanked him for being a nice man whom she would remember fondly. He escorted her to the car, she looked in the trunk, opened the bag and got an outfit and under garments, then locked the car. The two stood and talked about this being her first flight and how she was going to miss living in Rockville Center, which was so peaceful and quiet. As Kathleen was about to return to the building, an ambulance was turning the corner and pulled up in front of the apartment building. Two men with a gurney entered as Micheal ran over to open the door for them. A sinking feeling came over Kathleen. She ran inside, but seeing the elevator in use- she ran up the stairs. As she turned the corner past the incinerator, she saw several people standing and looking in the apartment- the Fasse's apartment. She pushed past the people and ran inside the apartment. There was Mr. and Mrs. Fasse holding each other as they watched Teddy being given oxygen and put on the gurney. "What happened," Kathleen yelled; "What's wrong with Teddy?" Kathleen was hysterical, and Mr. and Mrs. Fasse grabbed and held her. "We're going to the hospital." One of the neighbors offered to drive them as none were in any condition to do so. They put on some clothes as quickly as possible.

On the way, the Fasse's told Kathleen that Teddy had been ill, and they would explain later. At the hospital, the nurse met the Fasse's and Kathleen. She tried to stop Kathleen from going into the area where Teddy was, but Mrs. Fasse told the nurse that she was with them, and it would be alright. Teddy was hooked up to several tubes and was bleeding from his ears and nose. He was lying still, while the doctors took his parents aside. A moan came from Mrs. Fasse as she doubled over with what seemed like pain. The attendants set her down, while Mr. Fasse held her hand. Someone soon found a seat for him, as Kathleen never took her eyes off Teddy. His eyes opened and looked up at her and suddenly a sound went off, she was pushed away and doctors and nurses came around. Kathleen could hardly control herself as memories of her mother's death flashed through her mind. She ran out of the hospital, walking in circles and crying. An attendant came to see about her as she began to hyperventilate; then Kathleen fainted. When she came to, Mrs. Fasse was with her. Kathleen awoke with swollen eyes. She sat straight up in the bed and asked how Teddy was as Mrs. Fasse held her hand and shook her head. Kathleen cried aloud, "No, no...why, why!" Mrs. Fasse told her to please be quiet and to calm down or the doctor would give her a sedative. The little curtain was pulled back, and Kathleen saw Mr. Fasse comforting his daughter. Mrs. Fasse tended to Kathleen, "My dear, dear child, I... know how much you cared for him and how much he loved you. Maybe that's why I understood secrets, about who you really are. You see Teddy had one too. We told you about Teddy's injury to his head from the baseball bat. Well, it was after that injury that the doctors discovered inoperable brain tumors. He knew it, but he didn't want anyone else to know. He had been suffering so, and he kept it from you, because Teddy loved you so much, so much. Teddy wouldn't let any of us tell you either. We knew that this last trip we took was probably going to be the final one together-and he did not want you to see him sick; not ever. Your leaving was right on time. After we went into his room, he wanted you to go the next day." She stepped away from Kathleen and used a tissue before speaking again. "The doctors said that Teddy could have either become a vegetable or he could go the way he did. I...I hope that you won't get angry with us, if we don't take you to the airport today." The ladies held each other and cried.

Teddy's service was held the next day. Dorothy thought about funerals back home were held about a week after someone died, but not in New York; not with most Jews. Kathleen thought the ceremony short and quite civil, with a closed casket and no one fainting with grief. Dorothy attended and so did Lenny, a few of Teddy's Ham Radio friends and a lot of classmates from his school. Afterwards, a crowd gathered back at the apartment; everyone told funny stories about Teddy that made Mrs. Fasse laugh. Nothing could make Kathleen laugh. She had called home to tell her grandmother what happened, and that she would be coming home later. Kathleen could not see herself leaving Mrs. Fasse alone to tend to Teddy's clothes or things that he specifically wanted donated to charity and less fortunate children. Mr. Fasse was in a kind of daze at times, but managed to smile with family, throughout the evening. When the night was over, a silence fell on the apartment that left Kathleen without sleep until morning.

For about five days after Teddy's funeral, little or nothing was being spoken in the apartment, until one night Kathleen asked the Fasse's something, something that had been eating away at her. "Did I...I... cause Teddy to go sooner than expected? Please, tell me the truth." Mrs. Fasse's immediately wrapped her arms around Kathleen and assured her that that was not the case and not to blame herself for the inevitable.

Mr. Fasse went to his bedroom and brought back a photo album and asked everyone to sit around the dining room table. Mrs. Fasse poured tea for her husband, some wine for himself, and a cola for Kathleen served in their finest crystal. The album was full of pictures of Teddy, and they all talked for a couple of hours about him. Mr. Fasse stood and toasted his son and said, "I promised my son that each month after he passed on, we would talk about him, and never forget the good times. I thank God for my remarkable son, who taught me so, so much about love. That love is not selfish, but that you owe it to yourself to love yourself. That love is giving and it can never be taken away. Kathleen, Minnie, whatever the hell your name is does not matter to me. What does matter is that you're a good person, a good girl who loved and cared for our son, and he loved you." With a shrill in his voice, Mr. Fasse said, "And...and we love you too, Minnie-Kathleen." He smiled, hugged his wife, and touched Kathleen on the shoulder as he retreated to this room. Mrs. Fasse spoke after he left, "It is time for you to go home, my child. Teddy would want you to. You owe us nothing, you know, you just owe yourself happiness. Go home to your family, to other people who love you, too. Tomorrow or next week or whenever you say, we will get your ticket and you will fly." Just then Mr. Fasse opened the door, "Let's go, Betty. I'm sleepy." Mrs. Fasse touched Kathleen's face and retired for the evening. Kathleen straightened up the apartment and went to bed.

She decided it would be best to leave in about two days. Kathleen wanted to finish the packing of Teddy's things and call Memphis to get picked up at the airport- her first flight.

The next day, Kathleen made several calls-to her grandmother, to Ms. Clemmie, and to Ernest. The conversation ended with, "I'm coming home, Ernest, but I can't marry you, because I...I don't want to get married until I go back to school and get an education; ' be able to take care of myself. I need time with me, to find out what I can do for myself. I've got to go now." Kathleen didn't allow Ernest a chance to respond. She really did not want to talk too long to him or anyone else. If Ernest had called her back, she was prepared to ask Mrs. Fasse to tell him that she was unavailable. He didn't, but the phone did ring again. It was Dorothy asking if she could go to the airport whenever she was leaving. Kathleen asked Mrs. Fasse if Dorothy could go with them, and she agreed.

LaGuardia Airport was crowded, and Kathleen felt butterflies about the flight. Even so, she knew that this was also a part of her growth, riding in something that she thought of as a means of travel for the well-to-do, teachers, or someone important. Mrs. Fasse did not tell her what the ticket cost, but when they arrived at the gate, Mrs. Fasse handed Kathleen a very large envelope and asked her not to open it until she got on the plane. "I'm going to miss you, Minnie -Kathleen. But if you ever want to come and visit with us, just call. I can't imagine you as a housekeeper or live-in anymore. I think that you have great things in store for you. And please, remember what I told you about my family, me and-well, you know. You deserve the best, accept nothing less." Mrs. Fasse hugged her and told Dorothy that she would wait for her in the car. Dorothy spoke as she usually did, "Your white folks really love you." The girls laughed, and Dorothy continued, "Don't you want to open that before getting on? I know I couldn't wait." Kathleen shook her head and said that she would wait. Kathleen initiated the goodbye, "Let's get this hug over with. I'll call you when I get home. Shug, be good, and if you can't be good, don't be bad, okay?" Dorothy waved and Kathleen began running down the hall wiping her eyes. She thought about how Shug tries to be hard and cold, but deep down, Kathleen Shug had a warm heart.

The take-off was smooth, and Kathleen kept her eyes closed, chewed gum and swallowed like Dorothy told her to do; soon the plane leveled off. It was a non-stop to East Tennessee, then on to Memphis. Kathleen would not have to change flights, and she was very happy with that news. She looked around for safety, thinking about how to get out if she had to. Then she remembered that no matter what, she could do nothing if any disaster was to occur. So she settled down and decided to open the big thick envelope. Inside was a letter from Teddy. The words were sweet, telling of his happiness after meeting and getting to know her, and that no matter what happened to him, she would always be in his heart and hopefully him hers, and there was also a cashier's check for $3500 in Kathleen's real name. Teddy had requested that this be given to her upon his death to be used for her education or whatever she might need. He also wrote everything in Braille, with the translated one handwritten. Teddy wrote that he loved her, and that she should consider younger men like him for marriage-to which Kathleen laughed. Lastly, he ended with words of sorrow and forgiveness for not having given Kathleen her mail. Teddy was really jealous and chose to withhold them. Furthermore, Teddy paid Michael to retrieve the letters, which came once or twice a month. Teddy had gotten Michael to write his sentiments in English, which made Kathleen cry even more and smile.

The woman sitting next to her asked if anything was wrong. "No, no everything is alright, thank you." She looked further into the envelope and there were about a dozen letters addressed to her, unopened, but numbered. Only the one marked "number one" was opened. Kathleen was confused, but began to read them in their proper sequence. When she finished, Kathleen was quite shocked, but understood that if she had received those letters, she might not have stayed in New York as long as she did.

When the plane arrived in Memphis, Kathleen followed the path to claim her baggage. As she picked them up, she felt a tap on her shoulder and turned around to a very familiar face. "I've been here a while, and I actually thought that you might not really come," she said. He picked up the bags and began taking them to the car. He was walking with a slight limp, but did not seem too hampered by it. He opened the car for Kathleen and pulled off from the front of the airport staring from time to time at her. "I haven't been able to get you out of my mind ever since we talked. I just want to say that my intentions are not exactly honorable. I want to pull over, take off your clothes, take off my clothes and- yeah! But I'm a patient man; I can wait. Maybe until you make up your mind to marry me. When I wrote you, I at least thought that- Kathleen interrupted him and asked him to pull over to the gas station that they were approaching and he followed suit parking on the crowded lot. Kathleen moved closer to him, put her hands on his cheeks and kissed him softly on the lips. "I didn't know until I took that flight that all the time I was running, there was else someone running too, not away from me, but toward me. I don't feel…I don't want to run anymore. And I don't know for certain if I'm in love, but right now, I sho' have got a whole lot'a like for you. If I asked you, would you drive me someplace now, please? I'll explain on the way." Refusal was not even in his vocabulary. When they arrived, she looked around with teary eyes, got out of the car and ran to the back of the house.

Kathleen picked up a stick and a rock. She threw the rock in the air and hit it with the stick. She began to run to an imaginary base, and repeated the run to two other bases ending at home base- the place where she began. He looked at her adoringly, as Kathleen stood with her hands on her hips and tears strewing down her eyes. She looked around the yard where she had played for many years with her brothers, and their neighborhood friends. She thought of many things- her mother, school, how far she had come and where she was going. She thought of Teddy and his family, but mostly she thought of how her legs seemed to be a little bit longer; a whole lot stronger. They had taken her around the diamond; back to home plate. She thought of how it didn't matter that she could not run as fast as most, just that she had run enough to complete the game-the journey. Kathleen knew that coming home would put her on the next leg of the game, and that she was the wiser now for having played. All that she could ever be was her decision and not because of what man she had in her life. She found her own power within, and realized that she was now an experienced player in the serious game called life.

Frank walked up behind her, put his arms around her and held her tight. She turned, looking directly into his eyes, as tears rolled down her cheeks and said, "I have so much to tell you, about New York, and my friend, Teddy." Kathleen kept repeating "I'm safe, I'm safe, I'm safe..." as Frank held her tightly. She realized that Ernest would never have been a threat to Teddy, and he could never have written such letters or given her the respect that Frank thought she deserved. After Teddy got Michael to read the first letter that was sent, Kathleen understood that Frank's first letter impressed Teddy. He wanted Kathleen not to leave New York; not to leave him. Although he wanted Kathleen to be happy, he kept the letters addressed to her, and asked Michael to give him the mail whenever it came. Teddy was looking out for her in his own way.

Kathleen had traveled the course of the game's diamond-running away to the Big Apple an insecure young girl, unyielding on morals and understanding; flying back to Memphis a young woman enlightened; secure. She learned that love does not always come hand in hand with sex, (Mrs. Fasse), seeing is not only with one's eyes (Teddy), and morals and perceptions are not always common, (Dorothy and Lenny). Kathleen had jotted in her ledger/diary: "Geography notes location of a building or neighborhood where one resides, but no matter where you live, I know now that home never really leaves you." Finally, looking in Frank's eyes, Kathleen realized that she had made that "home run" that she always wanted to, and right next to her was that one man left on base.

The End

Printed in the United States
By Bookmasters